Henry Johnston

Doctor Congalton's Legacy

a chronicle of North country by-ways

Henry Johnston

Doctor Congalton's Legacy
a chronicle of North country by-ways

ISBN/EAN: 9783337230500

Printed in Europe, USA, Canada, Australia, Japan

Cover: Foto ©Andreas Hilbeck / pixelio.de

More available books at **www.hansebooks.com**

A CHRONICLE OF NORTH COUNTRY BY-WAYS

BY

HENRY JOHNSTON

NEW YORK

CHARLES SCRIBNER'S SONS

1896

TO

THE MEMORY OF DEAR FRIENDS

WHOSE PRESENCE NO LONGER BRIGHTENS

KILSPINDIE

CONTENTS

CONTENTS

DOCTOR CONGALTON'S LEGACY

ɪ

DOCTOR CONGALTON'S LEGACY

CHAPTER I

THE READING OF THE WILL

THE click and purr of the shuttle had ceased. No line of weft had been laid in the furrowed woof during that still and sultry afternoon. Tinny Walker's mallet was at rest beside squares of white metal on the workshop bench, and there was not even a quiver of heat at the chimney-head of the smithy. Nature, too, seemed in sympathy with the general cessation of human industry. It may have been the apathy of the listless air, but the twisted silver lines of the waterfall at the Brig-end, held together by a blue liquid film, fell more drowsily than usual among the lichened rocks. Sliding past, the river lipped its loamy banks with lingering gentleness, and fretted less than com-

3

mon at the intrusion of the bleachfield wall.
From nests that had served the season's purpose,
and that were now well hidden by the deepening
greenness, youthful and impressionable crows,
not having heard the kirk bell, rose and circled
over the scene in silent but questioning observation. No wonder, for being a healthy parish,
such occasions of week-day inactivity were not
frequent. The village of Kilspindie was scattered on two sides of the river Garnet, and was
held together by a three-arched bridge. The
bulk of it, including the kirk and the manse,
was on the same side as the general store. The
candle-maker's workshop stood at the corner of
the bridge on the other side, and was so situated
that Robin Brough, leaning over his half-door,
and looking up the acclivity to right or left on
such days as Gingham John, the packman, paid
his visits, could see him, with ell-stick in hand,
moving from door to door, and could guess with
a fair degree of certainty where he made sales;
and judge, from the houses at which he paused,
what the nature of the purchase might be. The
candle-maker was by habit a leisurely man, and
nothing loath at any time to suspend his frame

over the dipping-vat and indulge in surmises as to other people's affairs or gather the news from a passing neighbour.

The central situation of Brough's workshop, combined with the social disposition of its occupant, made the place a favourite rendezvous for such as had leisure to exchange views on the topics of the hour.

Robin pushed on with his tea without loss of time, and repaired across the bridge to the workshop in his white shirt-sleeves. Once inside, he closed the lower half of the door, and placing his elbows on it restfully, turned his eyes to the left. The mellow air was charged with the fragrance of hawthorn and apple-blossom. Ch-ch-ch-chir-ee, chir-ee sang the robin among the chestnut spikes overhead; but the candle-maker was not a thinking man, and did not bother with nature. His eye listlessly followed the white ascending road which ran for a space between green hedges. Further on to the right the sylvan wall was broken by a modest thatched building, in front of which swung a sign-plate, illustrating in appropriate colour that the designation of the place was the Wheat-

Sheaf inn. Higher still, a row of cottar dwell-
ings, with green house-leek shining among the
grey thatch, challenged notice, until at Nancy
Beedam's cottage on the one hand, and Broomfields on the other, the narrowing road cut into
another at right angles, and was lost to view.
At first there was no human object in sight,
but a flash of moving colour brought the gazer
back to the inn, from which a woman emerged
with a number of labelled bottles in a small
yellow basket. For a moment the unusual
sight of Mistress Izet, the housekeeper at
Broomfields, trafficking at the inn puzzled him.
"The lawyer will be biding for his denner," he
said. "I'se warrant the doctor's will has been
dry wark." Inference played an important part
in the knowledge they possessed of each other's
affairs in Kilspindie. As the housekeeper
passed, the sonsy form of David McLennan
appeared outside his own door, and seeing the
candle-maker at his post, he dashed the super-
fluous ham gravy from his mouth with the back
of his hand, and stepped down the brae. At
the lower end of the row he was joined by
William Caughie, who wore his Sunday stock,

6

and displayed one leg of his trousers partially caught up in the hurried fastening of his Blucher boot. William was a tall, slim, cold-rife man, who bore his head above the burly form of the carrier, and seemed to breathe a chillier air. Satisfied as to the approach of company, Brough glanced to the right without disturbing his pose of body. At the same moment Tinny Walker and Zedie Lawson made their appearance at the merchant's corner, and so they came, singly or in pairs, these rustic gossips, and planted themselves at the end of the bridge in front of the candle-maker's workshop. Each wore some remnant or other of his Sunday attire. Their manner, both of speech and movement, was characterized by Sabbatic leisure. That day they had laid the mortal remains of a notable member of the community in their last resting-place. A funeral in Kilspindie meant a day's idle-set to the male heads of families. On these occasions, there being time, the Seventh day's grace was said in full at breakfast. Adult male faces, lengthening for the melancholy duty in prospect, took a proportionately longer period to

shave. Dressing afterwards was done in leisurely stages, for on this particular day they did
not "lift" till one. While these preparations
engaged the attention of the men, the women-
folk with needle and scissors prepared crape-
bands for the hats, and "weepers" for the coat-
sleeves, with subtle appraisement in crape and
book-muslin as to the degree of respect to
which the deceased was entitled at the hands of
the wearers and their families. Work, as a rule,
was not resumed after returning from a funeral.
No native could account for this custom — it
had lasted as long as the memory could
stretch, and even steam and electricity had not
altered it much.

Dr. Congalton, whose remains had that day
been laid in the kirkyard, was one of the old-
est inhabitants. He had been for some time
out of practice, but was justly held in respect,
for he had stood single-handed by the portals
of birth and death of his rural constituency for
over thirty-five years, bidding welcome and
saying good-bye. The doctor was a bachelor,
and a person of uncommon individuality. Native gossip averred that he was once on the eve

of marriage, but the match was broken off on sanitary grounds. The lady's dresses were too long for his taste, and the chain of mutual regard could not stand the strain of his ineffectual desire to shorten them. Her feet had no need to shame her, 't was said, but he declined to bind himself for life to a person who not only trailed good things in the dirt, but made herself at the same time a circular receptacle for the seeds of trouble. Dr. Congalton's death was the result of an accident. Since his retirement from practice gossip whispered he had lived rather freely. At all events it was a fact, that one night, on returning from Windy-yett with his head full of whisky toddy, he drew rein for his own gate prematurely, was thrown heavily against a stone wall, and arrived home bearing injuries from which he never recovered.

Dr. Congalton, having enjoyed a long, undisturbed practice, was known to be wealthy, and while it was naturally supposed that what he possessed would go to his brother George, a journalist in London, an element of uncertainty had come on the back of this supposition by the news that Windy-yett had been invited to

the reading of the will. Richard Cowie, the
tenant of Windy-yett, was a keen and fairly
successful farmer, but outside of practical farm-
work he was, as his wife said, but a " puir stock,"
and needed " haudin' in." Mrs. Cowie possessed the power of doing this, and exercised
it. But those who were observant said she
could slacken the reins at times when it served
her purpose. Alec Brodie, the cartwright,
whose workshop was situated about half-way
between Broomfields and Windy-yett, and who
had opportunities of knowing, was responsible
for saying that it was her hospitality and her
management that drew Dr. Congalton so frequently to the farm, and her toddy, though she
could not be blamed for it, that "dottlit" him
on the night of the accident. A consuming but
smouldering desire to know something of the
destination of Dr. Congalton's belongings had
brought the neighbours to the Brig-end that
afternoon in considerable numbers.

Want of directness was one of the parish
failings. Tilly Brogan, the merchant, who came
from Motherwell as successor to Matha Spens,
was at first put off his guard by it. When

neighbours came to his store to purchase, their
desires were shrouded by a seeming of indifference, as if they were simply indulging a curiosity
to price things — beginning with articles they
had no mind for, and ending with what they
actually wanted — offering for it so much less
than was asked, as if shamed into purchasing
for decency sake, after giving trouble. As yet
the gossips were in the outer courts of inquiry
regarding what they had met to discover. Zedie
Lawson (his kirk name was Zedekiah, and he
knew this when his wife was angry) was sitting
on the edge of a candle-crate, looking skyward
over the bleachfield chimney, directed thither
owing to meteorological observations made by
the carrier some minutes previously. Zedie was
a stunted, timorous man, with a tilted nose, and
a mouth like the letter O. The expression was
apologetic, but to a stranger conveyed the idea
that he was whistling a tune; being short-
sighted, he was said to observe things with
" mouth and een." The look skyward, however,
was mechanical rather than indicative of exhaustive contemplation, for at the moment he was
in confused wonderment as to whether the new

laird of Broomfields would continue the services of his sister-in-law, Janet Izet, who had long acted as housekeeper to Dr. Congalton.

"Look nane anxious," was the masterful injunction given to him on leaving his own doorstep; "fin' oot things by degrees; let the crack come roun' nait'ral, and no clyte intil 't as if we feared Janet wud tyne her place." In the sequence of discourse the carrier had passed on to remark that the hay was requiring the sun "after that lang blash o' rain." Hairmyres had been telling him that the "feck o' his was cut this time last 'ear." He remembered it by "the bursting o' the dam, that carried half the meadow fu' o't into the Garnet."

"Hairmyres should mind it for better reasons than that," the little tinsmith took liberty to remark through his tin-trumpet of a voice. "His wife dee't a week after the dam broke — I have heard tell it was wi' fricht."

"It was fricht nane," remonstrated Brough, declaiming confidently from the half-door. "It was Buchan's *Domestic Medicine* that killed Jean Lowry. Dr. Congalton telt the schule-maister, and Mrs. Lonen made no secret o't to

my wife, that Jean Lowry read that book till
she had a' the troubles it speaks o', ane after the
ither, and whiles she had twa're three on her at
ae time."

"And like enough she wud be takin' med'cins
and stuffs that her system couldna staun',"
deplored William Caughie, looking sapiently
through his horn specs. William was great on
human organs and ailments. "Just that — she
took whatever the book said was guid for the
trouble she had on her mind at the time. What
mortal woman, or man either, could thole that?
I alloo the fricht wud help, but the doctor said
when he opened her it was nothing but Buchan
here and Buchan there, a' through her inside."

"It was mortal skilly o'm to fin' that oot,"
Lawson ventured, fondly hoping the colloquy
might now set on Broomfields.

"The doctor was an eccentric being," the
carrier said.

"That's about it," Jaik Short announced,
with approval. Short was the engine-driver
on the branch line. Trains had to be run, as
he said, in spite of fairs and funerals, and he
had come over from the junction, after stabling

his steed, to hear the news. "Eccentric's the word — a wheel wi' a hole in it nearer the tae side than the tither, put it on a rinnin spin'le, and, my word, it'll waggle. Lod, McLennan, ye never said an apter thing — the doctor was eccentric. Had ye a gran' funeral the day?"

"A big gathering," answered Robin Brough; "Gushets, and Harelaw, General Alexander, the factor, Robert Thomson, frae Glenbuckie, and ither big-wigs. The minister spoke real feeling."

"The accident was enlarged on — telt us to prepare, and the like," said William Caughie, working his nose. He was an elder.

"Talking o' big-wigs," interposed the tinsmith, attitudinizing to check sentiment, "the biggest in yon company the day, to my mind, was the undertaker's man. Gor! even the minister daurna open his lips till he says the word. At his nod the whisky gangs roun'. Everybody looks to him; but the tap rung o' his greatness is reached when he clears his throat and says, 'If ony body wants to see the corp before it's screwed down, come this wye.' Dod, Robin, if I wasna a maister tinsmith, I wud be an undertaker's man."

"There's no enough o' ye," said McLennan unfeelingly. The tinsmith, like some other little people, required keeping down. "That job wants a big, presentable, sober-looking man, like William Caughie. Still-an-on Walker, yer a decent wee fellow compared wi' yon shirpet body, the factor, wha walked wi' his nose i' the air as if he was immortal. It was oot o' place behind a corp. If that man was half as big as he thinks himself, he wud let oot for a saullie" (hired mourner).

Short had reason to have a different opinion of the factor, and changed the subject by asking bluntly if anything had been heard about the doctor's will. The engine-driver was not a native. Zedie Lawson jumped from the crate as if shot up by a spring. He felt things would be redd up now.

"I suppose the brither gets a'?" Short presumed.

"Windy-yett was invited to the reading," answered Brough. "There's no saying."

"He'll be a daer" (trustee), the engine-driver concluded. "Cowie and the doctor were great frien's. It'll no astonish me if he has left his siller to build a college for watching the staurs, or for telling what airt the win' blaws."

"Think ye Maister Congalton wud settle in these pairts gin he got the doctor's siller, as ye say?" Lawson's opportunity had come.

"Settle!" Short retorted, "did ye ever hear o' a newspaper man settling at the tail o' a junction? Na, na, if he settles it'll be somewhere on the main line, but Edinbro' or Lunnon's a mair likely place."

Lawson resumed his seat dolefully. The sister-in-law after all was to be thrown on them; surely she had as much saved as would pay them a weekly allowance for board and lodging till she got another place. This thought occupied him heavily till the smith arrived with startling news. That functionary had been driven off in Harelaw's gig after the funeral to see a beast that was suffering from pneumonia — peenumonia the parish called it; the schoolmaster had kept the smith right, being a professional man, but somehow the conviction remained even with him that the initial letter of the word was needlessly thrown away. He was telling how, when passing the cross roads near the cartwright's workshop on his way home, he met Windy-yett "swinging alang the gate in a terrible swither." The carrier planted his shoulder doggedly against the candle-maker's door-post.

"Ay, man."

"His mind wud be fu' o' the will," said Short.

"He was like a man clean oot o' the body," continued the smith. "Whiles he wud gie a hotch o' a laugh, syne he wud gang on a piece wi' his head doon, cracking to himsel' —— "

"But ye buckled to him?" interrupted the candle-maker.

"Man, he didna see me till I was three pairts into his long shadow that hurried on before him, but I stood; then he looked up at me wi' an eerie face. 'Getting foret, Windy-yett,' quo' I, wondering if he was in drink. Wi' that he raised his richt hand, brocht it doon on his knee, and hotched till the tears trinkled owre the nose o' him. 'Man smith,' says he to me at last, 'were you ever at the reading o' a will?' 'Na,' quo' I, 'but it maun be fine when ye're named in it.' 'Dod, I dinna ken, I can hardly say I've got the leeze o't yet; man, yon lang-nebbit, auld-

2   17

farrant words are by-ord'nar for senselessness. It was first party this, and second party that, and aforesaid the ither, till I was clean dumfoonert. Lord, I wis' the mistress had been there; but somehoo it rins in my head that the doctor has left his ain brither and the feck o' his siller to oor Bell.' "

CHAPTER II

THE OPINION OF COUNSEL

BROOMFIELDS was a substantial baronial building erected within about an acre of ground. It commanded a view of the village and the valley of the Garnet. There was a patch of lawn in front, broken at intervals by crescents and squares, in which pansies and white lilies were in the meridian of blossom. An old-fashioned garden behind, with gnarled fruit trees, common vegetables, and herbaceous plants justified the inference that the gardener, to be fully employed, must have other duties to perform. It was a beautiful June morning some days after Dr. Congalton's funeral. A soft shower had raced over the landscape, leaving a perfume of white clover and sweet-briar on the relapsing air. A blackbird out of sight somewhere among the blue-green palms of the

larch, refreshed by the moisture, gave evidence
of its simple joy of living in tones liquid and
melodious. Isaac Kilgour, perhaps the most
taciturn man in the parish, had paused in his
work with feet enveloped in a swathe of grass.
Mayhap 'twas to listen to the feathery poet
overhead, or to revel in the glorious feeling of
summer that pervaded the scene. One had to
put one's own interpretation on Isaac's moods.
It would be contrary to fact to say that economy
of speech necessarily betokens wisdom, though
thoughtful people, perceiving the unruly character of the tongue, will grant that there is
often wisdom in reticence. Isaac, however,
was wise to this extent, he did not allow
indulgence in speech to betray lack of knowledge. To Mistress Izet he was a perfect pundit,
nevertheless she was not slow to declare that
he was "a provoking craitur; for though he
heard and saw maist things, he never let on."
What his present thoughts were need not occasion concern, for they were soon interrupted.
He had mechanically inverted his scythe, the
handle resting on the lawn, and was wiping the
blade with a handful of grass, when an agile

collie, burning probably with the memory of some unrequited wrong, flashed past him like a bird-shadow, and next moment was in the throes of what seemed mortal conflict with Help, the house-dog, who was chained to his kennel in the garden behind. Isaac dropped his scythe, and, seizing a wooden-toothed rake with a safely long handle, literally but ineffectually hastened to tear the combatants asunder. The housekeeper, who was amongst the early vegetables catering for the mid-day meal, seeing Isaac's failure to promote amity with the rake, took up the broken handle of a spade, and laid on till her back ached ; but the blows added fury to the conflict, which seemed likely to terminate only with the life of one or other of the dogs. While Isaac was raking and Mistress Izet was belabouring, a small, bright-faced figure emerged from the kitchen door carrying a jug of cold water in her hand. This she proceeded to pour coolly over the writhing animals. In a moment the conflict ceased. The intruder passed the gate like an arrow, and Help, as precipitately, retired to his kennel, refusing to come out either to receive sympathy or show the injuries he had received in the encounter. Isaac looked at the housekeeper with the spade handle, and Mistress Izet gazed at the gardener with the rake, while the girl stood calmly smiling at the foolish attitude of both.

"Weel, I declare," said Mistress Izet, "if that wasna like a wumman in Houston parish." — Isaac was accustomed to the housekeeper's parallels from Houston parish, and stopped further palaver with a characteristic grunt.

"Umph'm," he said, wiping the perspiration from his brow with his sleeve, and speaking to the kennel: "That was clever."

"It was clever nane," deprecated the girl. "I've seen the keeper at Mossfennan doing the like mony a time. It's the only wye to pairt fechtin' dougs."

To their dismay they became aware that a gentleman was overlooking them from the study window, and that a bright child at his side was clapping her hands in recognition of the little maidservant's triumph. The party was dispersed by the ringing of the front-door bell, which the housekeeper hastened to answer.

"Eh, Maister Sibbald, it's you," she said, recognizing her late master's legal adviser, " I'm hardly presentable, being sair flustered wi' layin' on a couple o' fechtin' dougs. Come awa', ye'll find Maister Congalton i' the study."

She led the way up-stairs to that apartment, and taking the little girl by the hand under the pretext of telling her about the canine encounter, left the two men alone.

By his last will and testament Dr. Congalton had directed that his estate, with the exception of the house, which he left to his brother, was to be divided into three equal parts. One part was to go to his brother, and one part to his niece, Eva Congalton, while the remaining part was bequeathed to Miss Cowie, daughter of Richard Cowie, of Windy-yett, whom the doctor evidently intended his brother to marry, for there followed this important and significant stipulation, namely, should his brother marry while Miss Cowie was still a spinster, the whole estate with the exception of the house was to go to her. Similarly, on the other hand, should Miss Cowie marry while George Congalton remained single, her share was to be forfeited, and pass to Eva Congalton. In the event of any of the parties deceasing before marriage, the share of the person deceasing was to be equally divided between the remaining lives. Meantime, the estate had been committed to trustees, whose duty was to hold and conserve it for the legatees; but should his brother marry Miss Cowie, the trust was then to cease and determine in so far as the senior legatees were concerned, and their respective shares were to be placed entirely under their own control.

To do Mr. Sibbald justice, he had no sympathy with the doctor's whimsical disposition of his means. At first he had treated the proposal as a joke, due to some passing caprice, but the deed had remained unaltered. The doctor's thought, according to Mr. Sibbald, was that his brother should marry again, particularly for the sake of his child. He felt that the younger man's un-settled life as a newspaper free-lance afforded him few opportunities of mingling in the society of women, and the terms of the will had, he believed, sufficient suggestiveness to lead his mind in the direction of matrimony. As to the person intended for his wife, the will left little dubiety. 34

The doctor had been feasted and flattered not with the expectation of what had occurred, but in the hope that he himself might propose, and thereby bring the money into the Windy-yett family. It can hardly be said that either the farmer or his daughter realized the purport of these schemes. Windy-yett enjoyed the personal license and social amenities which his wife's hospitality to their neighbour afforded him. The habitual curb was on these occasions removed, and he jogged on happily with the driving rein resting lightly on his neck — that was enough for him. Bell simply and unconsciously acted the part assigned to her by the diplomatic head of the house. She was a rosy-faced, healthy, rollicking young person of about twenty. She had something of her mother's activity of mind and firmness of temper, but there was also her father's lack of worldly ambition, which Mrs. Cowie secretly deplored. Bell was tutored to be "blyth and couthie" to their guest, an injunction which thoroughly accorded with her own buoyant nature; and the exercise of these agreeable qualities during the doctor's visits had suggested the terms of his will. The trustees, of whom Mr. Sibbald was one, had, at the suggestion of the latter, taken the opinion of counsel for their own protection. This opinion was to the effect that the will was perfectly valid, and could not be set aside. Such was the information the lawyer had brought to Broomfields. Congalton had not doubted the result.

"The doctor's money is really an unimportant matter to me," he said smiling. "He had a perfect right of course to do what he liked with his own. But his humour was always of a grimish order, and this is part and parcel of the man. I remember the night before he died — he was comparatively free from pain — 'George,' he said, after beckoning me to his side, 'I have been thinking of you both — you and the bairn. You will see after I am gone how thoughtful I have been — philosophically thoughtful. I have not laboured and saved for nothing — money there will be, but I have endeavoured to put within your reach that which money cannot buy. Man, you will be surprised — you will think me a rare good fellow!' He lay back on the pillow; he was too weak to laugh, but the tears came into his eyes with the stress of inward merriment. 'You always accused me of want of sentiment,' he resumed, 'but I have put all the sentiment of my life into a nutshell, and now bequeath it to you.' Poor Harry!"

"I presume you have seen this young lady — this Miss Cowie," the lawyer inquired.

"No, I have not had that honour. Her mother, a bulky, loud-speaking woman, called several times during my brother's illness to inquire for him. She was full of professions of concern and maternal confidences. Nothing would do but that I should break the monotony of my stay at Broomfields by drinking tea with them at the farm."

"The doctor was not slow to inform me that the daughter is a 'weel-faured' dame and very presentable," the lawyer said, laughing. "It would be an excellent, or, as I might say, a curious coincidental joke if she caught your fancy after all."

"It would indeed," Congalton replied, not insensible to the humour of the thought; "but that is a contingency exceedingly doubtful.

27

My mind was certainly not tending in the direction of matrimony, but even if it had been, so contradictory is human nature, that my brother's good intentions have put marriage in that quarter out of the question. Let matters drift. Neither of us, I presume, is under compulsion to marry the other. As for me, if ever I should think of marrying, the thought of relinquishing poor Harry's money will not stand in the way. Meantime, I presume I am free to occupy this house?"

"Most certainly. In express terms of the will it is your own."

"That is so far well. As yet my plans are rather uncertain. I have a book of war sketches in the press, and other irons in the literary fire which will necessitate an immediate journey to London. Indeed, I shall be pretty much on the wing for some time to come. I should like, however, to leave my little girl in a comfortable home, to which I may return as occasion permits. Mistress Izet, I see, is an excellent housekeeper, and a motherly woman, but she is not exactly the kind of person to train Eva, nor would I like her to be dependent on the parish school for her education. She wants companionship, refinement, sympathy, but only a lady can judge of such matters. I am afraid I am taking a liberty, but if your wife, of whom I have heard my brother speak highly, would find a suitable person for the post of governess, it would be at once a great obligation and a relief to me." Mr. Sibbald was sure this would be a congenial task for his wife.

While the lawyer was on his feet, and ready to go, Mistress Izet came in and announced Mrs. Cowie.

For the moment Congalton lost sight of what humour the situation contained.

"What is the woman fussing about?" he inquired with ill-concealed annoyance.

"The visit may be congratulatory," said the lawyer; "or it may be the curiosity of her class, that lacks consideration for the time of business men. Though I should say, it is probable she has come to claim you as part of the doctor's legacy to her daughter. In any case, as I have no wish to be involved in delicate issues, permit me to wish you good-morning."

CHAPTER III

MRS. COWIE OF WINDY-YETT

RICHARD COWIE returned from the reading of Dr. Congalton's will with his ideas, as has been shown, strangely mixed. The invitation to meet the lawyer at Broomfields after the funeral naturally led his wife and himself to infer that they had somehow been named in the doctor's settlement. While the remark frequently made by the latter over his toddy at Windy-yett, that he would find a "guidman for Bell some day," only gave an evanescent brightness to the roses on Bell's cheek, and a passing fillip to the farmer's hilarity, it conveyed a deeper significance to the provident wife and mother. His sudden death had grievously marred her hopes. Yet here was a new element in the development of events which vastly stirred her curiosity. Mrs. Cowie was born to rule. As to management, she would have faced the National Debt;

30

but at obstructed crossings of purpose she was
subject to sudden ebullitions of temper. The
fibre of country life was not fine enough for her;
she felt she had thrown herself away in enter-
ing the nuptial state with a farmer who had
no ideas beyond the rotation of crops. More
than once her husband learned from her own
lips that she could have married a wool-broker,
and "might have had a leddy's life in town";
and more than once he secretly wished she
had. Her early desire, to atone for being a
farmer's wife, was that she might have a son.
Her plans were simple and clear. He was to
be a minister, and marry an heiress. His college learning would make him equal to the best
in the land, and, being his mother's son, would
ensure a good marriage. She thought of sitting
in the manse pew, or driving about the country
side receiving the respectful salutations of the
parishioners. The advent of a daughter, combined with the abandonment later on of all hope
as to a male successor, was cruelly disappointing,
and, while not modifying her aspirations, gave
pungency to her activities. When she got up in
the morning, and "put the nocks foret"—this

was Nance the dairymaid's way of stating the case
—"ye might be sure there was a touch o' north
i' the wind." The same authority, often tired of
unreasonable and vexatious service, said, " If she
(Nance) could only get into heaven by a back
yett she would be happy; but as for the mistress,
a front seat and a croon wud har'ly serve her."

Mrs. Cowie had sent Bell to her cousin's at
Brackenbrae with some "swatches" for summer
dresses, in order that she might have composure
to digest the news.

The smith's story at the candle-maker's workshop was no great exaggeration of Richard
Cowie's mental condition; and the leisurely
walk home between the fresh hawthorn hedges
had not materially aided the elucidation of the
doctor's intentions. The prevailing thought in
his mind was what he had communicated to the
smith, namely, that the doctor had bequeathed
"his brither and the feck o' his siller" to Bell.
He knew there was some complication about the
money being left in parts; but if Mr. Congalton
was to marry Bell, the litle girl would be Bell's
step-daughter, and consequently the whole of
the money would be in the family. This was

the sum of the information which, with much mental dubiety and confusion of terms, he conveyed to his wife. She was irritated, in her eager thirst for facts, at having to ask so many questions, and to find that he was either uncertain or in entire ignorance of many things she was dying to know.

"Supposing there is no marriage in the case," she said, after trying to encompass the idea of her daughter marrying a "widow-man." "Ye'll be able to tell me, I suppose, in round figures hoo muckle Bell's share is likely to be?"

"No; the lawyer didna say."

"But did ye no speir?"

"There wud be no gain in speiring, seeing the doctor's siller's in property and stocks. I suppose she'd get a third."

"Ay, and wha's to divide and see that justice is dune till'r?"

"Oh, it's to be boun' up some gate. Noo when I mind, it's to be i' the hands o' daers."

"Guid life! did ever onybody hear sic havers; if it's to be in the hands o' daers, the siller's no to come into oor hands after a'."

"Dod, I am fair bamboozled. I wis' ye had

3   33

been there yersel', that's what I said to the smith, but the minister 'll tell ye, he's ane o' them."

"And wha may the ithers be gin ye ken as much?"

"There are twa ithers in Airtoun besides the writer body himsel' — but bide awee, guid wife, whare are ye gaun?"

"Stracht to the manse, where I'll get the leeze o' things."

She was donning her mantle. Her keen desire for information had stirred the impulse which her husband's cooler nature checked, by reminding her that such eagerness "wud be gey ondecent, seeing the doctor's corp had only that day been laid i' the mools." That evening in the kitchen she made Nance long once more for a back entrance into heaven, but she judiciously avoided her husband and Bell.

Next day Mrs. Cowie repaired to the manse, and excused her own precipitancy by reflecting first on the lawyer for not being more explicit, and then on her husband for not duly inquiring after their lawful rights. She learned to her dismay that the minister had declined to act as one of the trustees. He knew the terms of the will generally, however, and explained that the remaining executors would hold the property in trust so long as Mr. Congalton and her daughter remained single, and that the interest only would be paid to the parties concerned. It was estimated that the doctor's estate would be worth about £20,000, at current prices of property and stocks. Her apprehension that the trustees might "make away wi' the siller amang them," was allayed by the minister's assurance that the will was registered, and that they would be bound to give count and reckoning whenever they might be called upon to do so.

She returned to the farm with a mind somewhat relieved, but diverted into new channels of activity. It was a comfort that Bell was provided for, though she should never marry; but, after all, what was to hinder her marrying as the doctor had planned? There were manifest advantages to her mind in such a union of interests. Mr. Congalton was a comparatively young man, and a gentleman; Bell would naturally rise to the position in society which she, the mother, had missed. At all events there was this £20,000. The man was used to a roving life. A person called upon to follow armies and write about great battles was engaged in a hazardous occupation, but that was his affair. She could see that proper settlements were made for Bell. There was also this tender "slip o' a wean," town-bred and puny, with no great legacy of health. If anything happened to her the siller would fall to the father.

Mrs. Cowie, for prudential reasons, only told her daughter that she had been remembered in the doctor's will. These dawning designs must be kept, even from her husband. She was not insensible to the fact that they were sordid and selfish. They had crossed her own mental survey of the situation naturally enough, however, and Bell's future was to be looked to. Mr. Congalton might be annoyed that any part of his brother's money was left past himself, but if any such feeling did exist she was sure it would pass away when he knew what good friends they had been to his brother, and how fond the doctor had been of Bell. Mrs. Cowie let the subject germinate, making mental estimates of the possibilities, and then set out for Broomfields. The question required management and delicacy of handling, but want of personal assurance in such matters could not justly be charged against her. Isaac Kilgour, whom she met at the gate, told her the lawyer was in. That was fortunate. She would ask a private word with him; there were questions still requiring explanation, which neither her husband nor the minister could make clear. She had asked Mistress Izet to announce her name; surely the lawyer would wish to be introduced to her as the maternal relative of one of the legatees.

There was a long pause, then she saw the man of law marching hurriedly away, and immediately Mr. Congalton came into the drawing-room, where she sat fondling his little daughter on her knee. For the moment she was disconcerted. Had these two men been conspiring against Bell? It looked like it. Mr. Sibbald had walked guiltily away instead of offering congratulations. The present was a crucial moment, and justified polite simulation. She acknowledged Congalton's greeting with her most captivating smile and her finest English. She was afraid her husband, who was rather shy, and at times absent-minded, had overlooked his duty, but it might be none the less fitting that she should call and put in words their satisfaction that any kindnesses they had been able to show to his late lamented brother had not been forgotten by him. It was an especial pleasure to her, that the remembrance of their long and neighbourly friendship had fallen in this sensible form on her daughter, whom he had known from bairnhood. Such a minding was altogether unexpected, and if there was any way in which they could show their gratitude to him or his daughter he was welcome to their services. Mr. Congalton was too well-bred to smile; he received these diplomatic sentences in a manner suitably gracious. He himself, he informed his visitor, was going immediately to London, and should be absent for some time on business.

He would not be taking his daughter along with him to such a place as London, she was sure. No; how glad she was of that. London was an ill place for tender, motherless bairns. Nor was Broomfields suitable either, with nobody but Janet Izet at its head. If he would leave the child in her care till he returned, it would give them some chance of showing the great respect they all cherished for the doctor's memory. Then she addressed the round-eyed, wondering child on her knee. "Ye'll see the horses and moos, and get a wee lammie to rin at your heels; the caller air o' the farm will bring flesh and colour to your bonny wee cheeks. Wudna ye like that?" Then the child would have in her daughter a refined and lady-like companion. Bell was daft about bairns, having no brothers or sisters of her own. Her daughter's boarding-school education in Edinburgh (she had been six months there "finishing" the scant tutelage begun and carried on for a time at the parish school) would enable her to foster and keep up the lady-like manners which nature and good upbringing had given her, but which she would be sure to lose if left to the housekeeper's unaided care. In thinking back on this interview, which she could not but regard as providential, her belief was unhesitating that a serviceable impression had been left, and that on the whole she had made the most of accidental circumstances. She remembered, but misunderstood what she called "the pleased glint" that came into his eyes at the mention

of her daughter's name; and the thoughtful way
in which he acknowledged the offer of their
services to his child. The intimation that he
had arranged to put Eva under the care of a
governess stimulated regret that she had not
been earlier in the field; but it did not last.
There was no harm in his having a brief trial of
a governess — her daughter had told her what
they were. At all events he knew now that she
and Bell were willing to assist and befriend him
in the upbringing of his daughter; and a crisis
was sure to come.

Mrs. Cowie lost no time in magnifying Mr.
Congalton's good qualities to her daughter.
"Such a ceevil-spoken gentleman, and such nice
soft eyes." Bell was like herself, impressionable, and might be led, but certainly would not
be driven. Ignorance of the doctor's intentions
towards Bell and his brother must, for a time
at least, be strictly maintained. She knew the
"contrairiness" of youth — a blunt intimation of
the facts might spoil all. The mother expressed
her belief that he was sure to marry soon, and if
she, Bell, cared for a grand marriage, with her
education and natural charms, there wasn't a

young lass in the parish would have any chance against her. The boarding school alumnus smiled at these flattering confidences. She was not yet conscious of having worked great havoc amongst the hearts of men. Willie Mitchell, a neighbouring farmer, and she had been casting "sheep's eyes" at each other of late behind backs. There was no positive love-making as yet between them, but she was on the seductive borderland of ideals, in which the sedate widower and the fresh young farmer could not fail to take places in striking contrast. This was apparent in her reply — she spoke laughingly.

"A proposal from Mr. Congalton would be a very funny thing," she said; "but when my time comes I want a young man or nane. If the doctor has left me siller, as ye say, I can afford to wait."

CHAPTER IV

SAUNDERS M'PHEE

THE REV. MR. HAZLET had preached his last sermon, and young Mr. Breckenridge, the newly-appointed successor, was to hold spiritual rule over the parishioners of Kilbaan in his stead. The elder man's hearers had no need to be shamed by their tears that day, for thirty-four years' tenure of the ministerial office had given him opportunities of being with them in the supreme moments of their lives. He had christened many of them and married most. He had followed the young and hopeful as well as the old and weary within the churchyard wall, and now the evening shadows were falling on his own autumnal day, and he felt the light had grown too dim for work. The hand-shaking was done mostly without words at the vestry door. Saunders M'Phee the school-master was the last to shake hands, and Andra Carruthers the beadle had come out bareheaded, having forgot to lock fast the Bible in the vestry press. They were standing side by side at the angle of the gable watching the diminishing figures of the minister and his daughters as they paced slowly down the brae past the cartwright's shed.

"Ay, ay," sighed Andra.

"Oh, ay," replied the school-master. There was a world of meaning in these simple words that required no explanations. There was no man in the parish like Saunders to Andra. They went back to the vestry before either spoke. The beadle closed the gown press with a bang and locked it to hide his feelings; then he went over to the Bible, opened it at the mark, and took out a small slip of paper — "All flesh is as grass, and all the glory of man as the flower of grass " — i Peter i. 24. He held it out to the school-master.

" No hauf a sheet o' paper," he said admiringly, "and yet he spoke for an hour and acht meenints."

"Man, man!" Saunders was not thinking of this feat of extempore eloquence, for he was advanced enough to approve of more paper and fewer words. His feelings at the moment were profoundly mixed, but what appeared to be uppermost in his mind had no concern with the sermon.

"Did he say anything about the degree?" Saunders inquired rather anxiously.

"Man, he did that; he showed me a letter from the Principal with the college seal on it. He seemed unco prood o't; but when I ca'd him doctor, he smiled wi' a kina thin smile and said, ' No, no, Andra, ye mauna change my name at this late hour o' the day. Sic honours *noo* are like dainties to a body in sickness, pleasing as a mark o' regaird, but like maist o' our worldly successes, come when the appetite to enjoy them has passed away. Besides, Andra,' says he, and the smile faded frae his lips, ' this honour costs siller, and is no to be thocht o' by steependless man.' "

The school-master walked through the village and up to the school-house with his hands behind his back and his head down. He was reviewing the elders one by one. Brinkburn, Meikle-Whifflet, Kilbeg, all men of substance, but they lacked his reverence for academic distinctions. What would they care for a short-lived honour that involved a siller payment. Saunders went indoors. The thing must not go abegging. He warmed his kail and took a frugal meal. He always made as much vegetable soup on the Saturday with the help of a shank bone as served for Sunday's dinner.

"Doctor Hazlet," he repeated several times, as if the sound gratified him. He took his Greek Testament and walked across the field behind the school-house, seeking the meditative seclusion of Balgrey Glen.

In some men kindness is like seed cast into an unresponsive furrow, apparently dead, but in point of fact only awaiting the springtime of opportunity. Twenty years before M'Phee, a broken and disheartened man, applied for the post of school-master to the parish of Kilbaan. He had the reputation of scholarship, but his views were reckoned unsound. Mr. Hazlet, then an able debater, fought his case through the Presbytery, and succeeded in carrying him to the dominie's desk. They had often differed since — at times bitterly, for Saunders was a

strong-headed man and dour in his opinions,
but deep down in his memory and out of human
sight he treasured this generous act of succour.
M'Phee read the Sermon on the Mount in the
original tongue, and returned with a set countenance for tea. He was a man of method, as
became a householder who had to do his own
turns. He washed the dishes, putting the delf
carefully away on the dresser, then he wound up
the clock, a duty he performed weekly after
sermon time. A look down the brae towards
the village was almost a needless precaution, for
the heads of families who were on visiting terms
with him always spent an hour in harkening
"questions" before taking "the books." Still
he wanted to make sure of privacy. Hearing
the voice of singing in Sam'l Filshie's satisfied
him. He went in and shut the door — the sede-
runt might be a long one, so he brought his
stuff-bottomed arm-chair and placed it in front
of the chest which sat in the window recess.
The westering sun glinted green among the
shiny folds of his well-worn Sunday coat, which
he had carefully put away before dinner. The
body of the chest served as his wardrobe, but

the "shuttle" was reserved for other purposes. This was his treasury — his sacred chamber — which was only approached half-yearly when he received his salary. He raised the hinged cover, and rested the lid of the chest on the upper edge of it. Here were the souvenirs of a lifetime, of little intrinsic value, but telling to those who could understand, of brief triumphs, tender hopes, and bitter disappointments. A gold medal, a packet of letters written in an ill-formed feminine hand, a lock of dark hair tied with a pink ribbon. He passed these reverently to one side, and came upon an old college Calendar lying beside some class tickets bearing the imprint of the University of Glasgow, a parchment certificate on which was written, "Alexandrum M'Phee," marked the place where the regulations for conferring degrees were printed. He had taken this M.A. degree after sore travail twenty-two years ago, and sold his Greek Lexicon to assist in paying the fees. The journey between M.A. and D.D. had at one time occupied his own day-dreams and seemed an attainable possibility, but it had ended at the desk of a parish school.

"D. D." He came to the place at last. He had never previously arrived at the practical point of contemplating the fees payable for this honour. He felt it was a graceless ordinance, and unworthy of a college of learning that a man deserving such distinction should be placed in a position to decline it for a reason he would not own — his poverty.[1] He laid aside the Calendar and opened a little inner drawer; this was the strong room of his treasury, containing the savings of his later lifetime. Among the small heap of sovereigns there was a well-worn marriage ring and a brooch. These indicated more than sentiment: they belonged to his mother. There was also a newspaper cutting giving a report of Mr. Hazlet's defence of the school-master before the Presbytery. The paper was well worn and yellow with age. Its terms were burned into his memory, but he read them again.

"We've had our differences," he said; "he's a perfect fule body in mony things. To threep on me that the Theory of Ideas was formulated by Plato — and as for Arminius, the minister's

---

[1] The fees for honorary degrees in Scotland are now abolished.

reasoning stands on feeble legs before Limborch, Le Clerc, and Welstein, still — an — on —— " He thrust his hand in among the sovereigns and counted one, two, three, four, up to twenty. He shut the lid of his treasury and locked the chest. Then he rose and placed the sovereigns under his pillow.

Later in the dusk of that June evening, after he had sung four verses of the 2nd Pharaphrase, he addressed the Deity on his knees. It could hardly be called a prayer — it was rather an expositorial statement of his feelings, the intensity of which demanded the vernacular to give it fitting expression.

"It's no Plato — it's no Aristotle — though in spite of what the minister may say he has the richt grip o' the Theory of Ideas. It's no that man Calvin, nor yet Arminius, — still wi' reverence be't spoken, the latter, to my mind, understands Thee best, — but it's Thoo Thysel' we have to do wi', and in Thy sicht we are puir craiturs at the best, D.D. or no D.D. This worldly honour has fair ta'en my haed. I had early set my ain hert on't, but, as the Psalmist says, ' Remember not the sins of my youth; ' since it canna come

to me let it fa' to the minister.   He canna tak'
a broad survey o' truth like Arminius, but he
was the instrument in Thy hand o' doing me a
good turn when my enemies, perfect Bulls o'
Bashan, were like to destroy me.   As for Andra
Carruthers, I like him weel, but he is a puir
stock — naira, naira, even nairaer than the minister; but he'll maybe mend under this new Mr.
Breckenridge — let us hope the best for him.
Whatever happens, may ' Thy Kingdom come,
and Thy will be done on earth as it is in
Heaven,' and that'll mak' a michty change.
Amen."

CHAPTER V

THE GOVERNESS ARRIVES AT BROOMFIELDS

NO one ever knew the sacrifice Saunders M'Phee had made, but the minister got his degree. He had relinquished the manse for a small cottage and a meagre retiring allowance. Such social catastrophes leave little room in practical minds for sentiment. The household consisted of the minister, his wife, and two daughters. Their slender income might with thrift serve for three, but a fourth would straiten it for all. This view had no place in the thoughts of the parents, but to the daughters it was present from the moment the door of the manse had closed behind them. Hetty, the younger, was the more accomplished of the two. She had a good English education, spoke French and German, played and sang, and had some knowledge of painting and drawing. As yet no

51

one, with the exception perhaps of her sister Violet, knew the mental force and moral fortitude of this gentle, dark-eyed little woman. She was full of resource, and capable of the most complete self-effacement in the interests of those she loved. It was she, therefore, who resolved to face the world and seek independence for the family good. Nevertheless it was not without silent tears, and a keen sense of impending separation that she sat down to respond to Mrs. Sibbald's advertisement in the county newspaper. Two days afterwards a letter was received inviting the applicant to an interview. For a brief space the family serenity was disturbed. The parents, for obvious reasons, had been kept in ignorance of the schemes that were taking shape in the minds of their girls. They were not insensible, however, to the kindness of their purpose, and to the practical wisdom of the steps they had taken when these became known. The interview was satisfactory on both sides, the inevitable breach in the home circle was made with as little fuss as possible, and with a brave heart the little governess responded to the call of duty which led her to Broomfields.

Eva Congalton was a pale, sweet-faced little girl, gentle, sensitive, and exceedingly impressionable. At the age of six she lost her mother. Immediately thereafter she was placed under the care of a maiden gentlewoman who kept a school for girls in Kent to supplement an income rendered inadequate for her own maintenance by the extravagance of a prodigal brother. She was nearly two years under Miss Vanderbilt, but, being most of the time in delicate health, had learned almost nothing systematically. She could read and write indifferently, was rapid at mental arithmetic, but woefully deficient even in the rudiments of religious knowledge. Her father, who was the son of Scottish parents, was educated in Scotland, but he had revolted against the Scotch system of cramming the young mind with dogma and doctrine before it was capable of understanding their meaning. His daughter's religious training, or want of it, was the result of this revulsion. Mistress Izet's trustful and simple orthodox mind was on more than one occasion sorely disturbed before the governess came. To her this little girl was a deplorable phenomenon — a harassing

enigma which puzzled and vexed her. While
Eva's health had not permitted her to pursue
any systematic course of lessons, she had picked
up scraps of the information which Miss Vanderbilt lavished on her girls.

One day while the housekeeper was engaged
preparing dinner, Eva, who was turning over the
leaves of a picture story-book beside her in the
kitchen, suddenly inquired —

"Where is Agricola's Wall?"

"Wha's wall?"

"Agricola's."

"Wha was Agricola?" inquired the housekeeper, taking a glance at the child's book —
"Div ye see't there?"

"Oh, no, he was a Roman, and built great
walls. Miss Vanderbilt said there were some in
Scotland."

"Chaipels, likely," retorted Mistress Izet
dryly. "Scotch folk dinna like the Romans —
they are maistly Irish, and no to be lippened
till."

"I don't understand," said the child, tossing
the sunny hair out of her eyes, and looking
puzzled. "They built great walls."

"I wudna say; they are mason's labourers and the like for the maist pairt; but wait till harvest time, and ye'll see great droves o' them raking through the county seeking shearing." This was very different from the character given to them by Miss Vanderbilt, and Eva looked as if there was some misapprehension — some discrepancy. "They are folk wi' a different religion frae us," further explained Mistress Izet.

"What is religion?" queried the child, innocently.

"Preserve us the day — does the wean no ken what religion is?" She had only found a parallel once to such ignorance in Houston parish but she suppressed the exclamation. "Did that Miss Vanderbilt you speak o' no gang to the Kirk on Sabbath day?"

"What is the Kirk, and what is the Sabbath day?"

The housekeeper threw up her hands and dropped eyes of pity on this precocious item of heathendom. "Puir bairnie," she said, gazing tenderly on the motherless outcast, "it's time we had ye at your Question Book. The Kirk is God's hoose — the Gates o' Zion; and the Sabbath is the Day o' Rest — the Lord's Day, when we cease frae oor labours — ' for in it thou shalt not do any work, thou, nor thy son, nor thy daughter, thy man-servant, nor thy maid-servant, nor thy cattle, nor the stranger that is within thy gates, for in six days the Lord made heaven and earth, the sea, and all that in them is, and rested the seventh day: wherefore the Lord blessed the Sabbath Day and hallowed it.'" Mistress Izet ran herself out of breath to insure continuity. She had committed the words to memory when a child, and feared now that any pause might lead her to mix them up with other catechetical answers which still lingered in the recesses of her memory. "Ye see ye're forbidden to work on the Sabbath day."

" Oh," cried Eva, brightening with comprehension, " that would be like the day we had no lessons. We called it Sunday, and Miss Vanderbilt went to chapel."

" Puir lammie! What an upbringing for a child," thought Mistress Izet. This accounted to her mind for the question about the Roman wall, clearly some Jesuitical way of talking about a Catholic Chapel. From that time forward the simple and honest housekeeper drew largely upon her store of biblical and other knowledge, to counteract, if possible, the baleful influences of Miss Vanderbilt's neglect.

One night before the arrival of the governess, Mr. Congalton, in passing his daughter's bedroom to his own, heard suppressed crying. On going in he found the child sobbing under the clothes, and her pillow wet with tears.

" Eve, darling, what is the matter? " he inquired in serious concern.

" Oh, papa," she cried, putting her arms round his neck and hugging him close, " I am so unhappy because I have got no lamp."

" A lamp, my dear child, what would you do with a lamp? "

" Mistress Izet says we must all have lamps like the wise virgins; and if we are good we must have oil in them, so that when the bridegroom comes at night we must light our lamps and go out to meet him. Oh, papa, I am afraid if I have no lamp and no oil, I shall fall in the dark, and not get into heaven at all."

" My dear child," he said, seating himself on the bed and wiping the moist cheeks tenderly,

"that is a very pretty story of the marriage customs in an eastern country" — he recapitulated
it simply and briefly, — "but there are no such
marriages here. Mistress Izet meant you to be
a good little girl, and always to do what is right;
but it is all nonsense about oil and lamps and
going out at night in this cold, miserable climate
of ours."

"Then I need not have a lamp, papa? — I
would like so much to get into heaven."

"You need have no fear of getting into heaven,"
he said, smoothing her sunny hair, "and when
you go God will take you there in the light. But
you must go to sleep now, and grow big and
strong, for papa wishes to keep his dear little
Eve to himself for a long, long time."

"But I am trying very hard to be good," she
said brightly. "I am learning the Question
Book. Oh, papa, can *you* say the 'Chief end of
man'?"

Curiously enough Mr. Congalton had a talk
that afternoon with the school-master on the
stern and exclusive character of religious beliefs
in the Scottish Church. "What are creeds for?"
he had inquired, "but to make their believers

Christ-like. If a man's life is pure, unselfish, and devout, do not despise him because of his creed, or albeit he professes none, for creed may be the husk of hypocrisy."

The unconscious humour of the child's inquiry brought a momentary smile to his lip. " My darling, your head must not be troubled with these things now," he said gravely; " I must forbid Mistress Izet giving you any more lessons."

" But, papa, don't scold her, for — for you don't know what might happen — perhaps she might wish to die."

" Nonsense, Eve, why do you suppose such a thing? "

" Because, papa, she told me last Sunday that all good people are — oh — so happy after they die; and if you were to be angry with her she might wish to leave her place and go to heaven."

Mr. Congalton made no further remark, but tucked the clothes in snugly about the little shoulders, and soothed her with his presence till she fell asleep. His remonstrance with the housekeeper was firm and final. Mistress Izet felt, considering the child's benighted condition, that her zeal had been but ill-requited, and retired to the kitchen indulging a frame of mind which constituted a sufficient barrier to the immediate translation which Eva feared.

One morning some days afterwards the father was startled by Eva's sudden appearance in his study. She had been so restless at night that he had given the housekeeper permission to sleep with her, carefully forbidding conversation on religious subjects. There was an expression of mingled regret and pleasure on her face as she stole up to his ear and whispered —

"Mistress Izet will not want to die *now*." Then her eyes darkened. "Oh, papa, do you know she is a very wicked woman!"

He put down his proof-sheets, and looked earnestly into the troubled face — "No, Eve, I do not think she is a very wicked woman. Why do you say so?"

"Because I heard her speaking to some one in the middle of the night," she replied. "I looked out of bed, and saw her on her knees at a chair. She said, oh, such dreadful things about herself that I was afraid. She was a worm — all wounds and — and bruises — deceitful — dreadfully wicked, and — such a lot more."

This was a sacramental period. Janet always abased, if she did not abuse herself miserably in her prayers about Sacrament time.

" My dear," he said, " Mistress Izet is a really good woman. Perhaps she had a bad dream and was speaking in her sleep. People sometimes speak in their sleep when they are dreaming, and say things they don't mean, and that are not true." He understood, but how could he explain to a child? It was clear to him, however, clearer now than it had ever been before, that his daughter required other tuition and other companionship.

From the first Eva took to her governess. They had lessons in the morning, rambles in the fields and green lanes before dinner, music, sewing, and games in the afternoon. She was wonderfully methodical, this little daughter of the manse — everything in its order, but nothing overdone, always leaving off while there yet remained a mental appetite for more. Mr. Congalton wrote regularly to his daughter, and encouraged her to write to him in return.

These letters were always submitted to Hetty for revisal, and as often as not they required it. This is what she brought one day for approval.

" Dear papa, wunt you come hom when the buke you told me about is finished? It wood be so awfuly nice to have you at hom. You could go with us to the woods, and other nice places. Miss Hetty wood tell you all about the wild flours and things. She knows such a lot. My dear papa she must allways stay with us. I am sure you wood like her so mutch you wood never go away agane. We went to the farm yesterday — the one with the funy name — Mrs. Cowy was allways asking us. We had scons and milk, and then she toke me to a rume by myself and asked if I was hapy, and if I was not tirred of lesons. Then she said wood I not like a nice kind mama, but I told her I was never tirred with my lesons, and wanted only Miss Hetty and you." The child's eyes sparkled with anticipation of approval. She was quick to apprehend looks.

" What, will it not do? " she inquired as she saw Hetty's flushed face.

" No, Eva dear, it is very kind, but you must

not speak of me thus to your father. Then it will not do to report gossip, you know — Mrs. Cowie was very good to us."

"I do not like Mrs. Cowie," said Eva firmly; "I — I don't think she is a lady."

"Oh, Eva, that is not like you."

"I am sorry — but I did not tell you all — she said something about you —— "

"Oh, country people are outspoken sometimes," Hetty interrupted, "and do not quite mean all they say. You must not allow yourself to think ill of Mrs. Cowie. I am sure your father would not like us to talk about people unkindly. Come and let us try again."

They took hands and danced laughingly back to the school-room, where between them the letter was recast — as it had much need to be — in less suggestive terms.

CHAPTER VI

A NARROW ESCAPE

To Hetty Hazlet the new life at Broomfields was a busy one, and brought with it the happiness that accompanies useful activity. Now and again Eva would startle her teacher by questions as to the action of the moon on the tides, the people who live in the planet Jupiter, the kind of breath the flowers breathe, and other matters suggestive of Miss Vanderbilt; but Hetty discouraged all irrelevant discourse by telling her that, interesting as these subjects might be to the elder girls for whom her early teacher intended them, she could only reach and know them by diligently following the course of instruction now prescribed for her. The thirst for higher knowledge was thus made an incentive to overcome the rudimentary difficulties that formed her every-day task.

Hetty's influence, exerted primarily in the school and play-room, soon radiated and filled a wider circle. Mistress Izet had so long been without a rival in the house, that naturally the presence of the governess was at first a trifle disturbing, probably from her fear of divided authority. But when she realized that this authority applied only to the child, and saved her the ordeal of answering embarrassing questions, she breathed more freely. Before the advent of the governess Mrs. Izet complacently thought she could give a good reason for her own simple faith, but the child's eager and puzzling inquiries when the housekeeper came to close quarters with herself stimulated humility. Hetty knew her place, and kept it with prudence. Her comings and goings were cheerily sympathetic. Association with refinement had been no part of the elder woman's experience, and Hetty's courteous, practical manners soon won her confidence. Trust once established makes the reception of new ideas easy: Mrs. Izet learned many things from the governess without awaking the consciousness of being taught, so it happened in time that the younger

5

woman, not by assumption, but by the inevitable influence of the superior over the inferior mind, became practically the controlling spirit of the house. Isaac Kilgour, on the other hand, stood apart in his superior masculinity. He regarded the new-comer as probably a suitable mentor and companion for his master's child, but he had not an exalted opinion of her sex generally. He was not unconscious that they became wonderful creatures sometimes in books, but he felt that that was largely the outcome of imaginative minds. For his own part he had never yet met the woman he could canonize. That they were useful, almost essential to man's well-being in the minor details of life, he was willing to concede, but that they were also at the root of most of his moral ills and perplexities was borne in upon him by his own observation. Isaac lived in a single apartment above the coach-house. His sole companion was a parrot. It had capacity for speech, but all it could say when it came to Broomfields was — " Irr ye there? " He got it from a Paisley man, who plumed himself on the purity of his accent. The bird was no favourite with the housekeeper, but she, in her comings and goings, was unconsciously responsible for most of the words it knew. Isaac reasoned that this accounted for " the bruit's ill-tongue."

The gardener was a hale man all week round, but had rheumatics on Sundays. The main cause of this ailment was his distrust of the minister. It was then the bird and he had their sweetest communion.

"It's no muckle to look at," Mrs. Izet was saying to the governess as she took her and Eva up to Isaac's quarters one day in his absence, " but it has an oncommon tongue." The parrot was a small ash-grey bird about the size of a pigeon, with a broad crimson tail. The housekeeper's voice startled the creature into activity. It made a sudden circuit on the upright wires of the cage, threw a somersault, and alighted again on its ring with an interrogation in its eye. To the housekeeper its supreme impudence seemed to say, as its master might have done, "Can ye touch at that, Janet?"

" Pretty Poll," said Hetty, looking with kindly eyes through the bars. The bird jerked its head on one side to think of this fresh voice. The words were unfamiliar — it was not accustomed to flattery.

" Pretty Polly, you might speak," Eva added coaxingly. The parrot tossed its head and turned up a meditative black eye, as if committing another tit-bit of musical articulation to memory.

" Fule craitur," Janet remarked tartly. "What ails ye, glowerin' that gate, without a word? Ye can chatter enoch whiles when it's no wanted."

" Isaac —" cried the bird, blinking hard — " Isaac — irr ye there ? — Here's Janet — nesty cuttie." Eva screamed with delight.

" I declare ye wud think the beast was human — I never hear its voice but it puts me in mind o' a wumman in Houston parish — she had an awesome gift —— "

" O' bad language," interrupted Isaac, who had come quietly on the scene, and completed the remark after his laconic fashion.

The vulnerable spot in the gardener's armour of indifference was the parrot. They once had a parrot at the manse, Hetty told them, and she narrated amusing stories of its antics. Her uncle in Glasgow had a starling that had an extraordinary gift of speech, and could sing " Up in the morning's no for me — up in the morning ear — ley." Hetty imitated the bird's tone and manner to Isaac's delight. She also informed him that West African parrots had been known to live for a hundred years.

" D'ye hear that, mistress? " Isaac eyed the housekeeper gleefully.

"Oh, that'll please ye fine," she replied with a laugh ; "but, my surce, he'll leeve a heap less than a hunner years gin he be na taught to keep a cecviller tongue in his hacd."

Isaac's regard for the governess, stirred at first by her interest in talking birds, ripened by fuller intercourse. Her knowledge of botany and flower culture was a source of wonder to him. He would stand by silent while she discoursed to her pupil on the nature, habits, and structure of flowers. He believed she could name them all in Latin as well as English. It may be supposed that the gardener had got pretty well beyond himself, and was on the way to a higher estimate of woman-kind when he confided to the housekeeper that that Miss Hetty " was a by ordn'ar lass : no content wi' birds and garden-flowers, she had e'en set to in his hearing and made a grand thing oot o' a sheuch o' weeds."

Hetty's scheme of education for the child embraced nature as one of its class books. This wholesome branch of study was taken every day when the weather was propitious, but Saturdays were their gala days. Isaac gradually became interested in these excursions. He himself suggested a visit to Crosby Glen, and on a bright Saturday morning personally escorted them thither. " Ise warrant ye'll have plenty to talk about till denner-time," he said, as he left them at Park-yett gate. A small brown road, veined and knotted with roots, led them into the bosky depths of this umbrageous place. It was a scene in which nature ran riot in the exuberance of her occult forces. In mossy hollows, at the roots of spruce and larch, lingering primroses peeped from their encircling leaves like eggs in their soft green nests, startled rabbits darted hither and thither, and lo, as if to illustrate the lessons of the week, a large brown squirrel paused in its ascent of a syca-

more to scan the intruders, and give them
leisure to admire its grace and beauty. The
eye and ear of the child found grateful surprise
at every turn. The flutings of birds; the soft
tenor of the bee; the velvety yellow-green of
the moss; lichened boulders, half buried in the
lush undergrowth of bracken and grass. Sharp
lines of sunshine sliced the sylvan gloom, gild-
ing root and bole. An ancient trunk, with
snake-like roots turned skyward, bore a slender
aspen whose leaves twittered joyously above
the ruin on which it flourished. In the hollow
the stream gurgled dolefully out of sight. Eva
was fascinated by the vast, dome-like magnifi-
cence as well as by the minute beauty of the
objects around her. Inquiring enthusiasm gave
little pause to the teacher. This infinite wealth
of greenery through which they waded, how
marvellously fashioned in detail? The hemlock
with its pinkish-white coronet of flower; the
graceful corrugated leaves of the despised
dock; bending spindles of grass swaying under
a weight of tasselated silver-grey flowers; the
wild hyacinth, now entirely denuded of leaves,
bearing its shiny globes of seed above the
encroaching grass.   71

To the imaginative Eva this was a memorable afternoon, but the recollection of it was grimly impressed on the minds of both by the almost tragic occurrence that brought it to a close. Returning home through the Crosby meadows, they were alarmed by the angry bellowing of a young bull at a barred space in an adjoining field. Hetty seized her pupil's hand, and had barely run a dozen steps when they heard the barrier giving way. The governess directed their flight to the nearest refuge — a dry-stone dyke, lifted the child in her arms, and dropped her safely on the other side. She had not time, however, to save herself, for the infuriated animal was at her heels, and ere she knew tossed her out of further harm's way over the wall. Fortunately McLennan the carrier was on the brow of the hill road returning to Kilspindie, and saw the race as well as the subsequent disaster. In a few minutes he was on the spot, for he stopped Brownie and ran. Hetty was stunned, but soon regained consciousness. Her foot was sprained by the fall, and as she was unable to walk, McLennan took her up in his strong kindly arms, carried her to the cart, and

conveyed her and her charge safely home. In
addition to the sprain she was slightly gored in
the arm, but made light of the injury, and
begged that it might not be spoken of lest an
exaggerated account of the incident should
reach and alarm her parents. This injunction
of silence was too much for the honest carrier.
The air in these slumberous by-ways did not
often vibrate with real adventures. Yet here
was an adventure in which he himself had borne
a chivalrous part. It was not every unmarried
man who could boast truthfully of carrying
a full-grown young woman in his arms over two
and a half acres of ground without resistance.
The thought fired his imagination, and made
him think of the days of knight-errantry. He
longed to tell it to Alec Brodie, who would
probably make a "po'm" about it. In fancy
he had already crowned his heroine with the
nimbus of a heroic deed.

" No tell ! " he said to his sister; " gey like !
It was her modesty. But what I'll tell will be
to nobody's disadvantage. If Robin Barbour
sen's owre for that bag o' tenpenny nails ye'll
fin' me at the candle-maker's workshop."

CHAPTER VII

WINDY-YETT MAKES A MISTAKE

IT was Sunday afternoon before the news of the accident reached Mrs. Cowie. There was little else talked of by the men in the kirkyard before sermon time. It was not the habit of the women-folk to palaver in this outer court. They went at once to their high-backed pews to compose their minds, and see what their neighbours had on. Mrs. Cowie's active mind took in all that was worthy of observation at a glance, and her eye travelled out of the loft window to where the cadger's horse was cropping the scant grass. She was marvelling at the absence of Janet Izet, and her "so set up wi' her mournings," but this was made plain to her afterwards at "skarling" time, on their way down to the inn where they had "lowsed."

74

"Just you taigle awee in yokin'," she said, when her husband had finished his story. "I'll run up to Broomfields and see if the bairn has been hurt."

"Tschah woman, ye needna fash, for they tell me she won aff withoot scaith."

"Will ye no do as I tell ye?" she replied hotly, "some men'll never learn sense. Wud it no look gey heartless efter what has come and gane if I didna see till the bairn in her father's absence? Whare's Bell?"

It occurred to Mrs. Cowie at the moment that her daughter's company on such an errand might serve a good purpose. But Bell had preferred to walk home with some young friends, and Richard Cowie, hurrying on to overtake the carrier, felt there was leisure and opportunity for a dram while his wife was making her ceremonious and diplomatic call.

"There's that woman Cowie," exclaimed Mistress Izet, jumping to her feet and all but overturning a plate of hot "kail." She, Isaac, and Jenny Guililand had sat down to dinner in the kitchen (Isaac always dined there on Sundays). "Jenny, rin and shut the door of

the drawing-room. Show her into the parlour
and dinna open your lips, guid or ill, till
I come; we'll gi'e her no occasion to
clype."

When the housekeeper returned she reported
what had taken place as she served out the
sheep's head.

"Speirin' body," grunted Isaac, helping himself to potatoes.

"Guid forgie me for leein," said Mistress Izet,
the spur of remembrance touching the side of
her conscience. "When she asked to see Miss
Hetty hersel', I said she hadna sleepit a wink
a' nicht wi' the pain in her fit, and that the
bairn and her had just lain doon thegither and
were fast asleep. That was an awfu' lee to tell
on the Sabbath day, Isaac, when they were baith
sitting at their denner i' the next room. Jenny
Guililand," cried the speaker, suddenly realizing
her indiscretion, "if you tell a word I'll — oh, I
dinna ken what I wud do — I'll — I'll just — tak'
the haed aff ye!"

"Um," interjected Isaac, ignoring the intimi-
dating parenthesis, "what said she syne?"

"Oh, she then commenced to black-ball Miss

76

Hetty for her want o' sense in taking the bairn into places o' danger; but I coupet the tables by saying it wud be wicer like if she got her ain guid-brither to put a halter on sic vicious bruits, and tie them i' the byre-en', instead o' letting them rampage aboot terrifyin' the lives oot o' simple folk. Nothing wud do but that the wee lassie should be sent up to the farm for a few days to settle her nerves."

"To get the news, and breed mischief," said Isaac, taking a trotter in his fingers — having exhausted the capabilities of knife and fork.

"Just to breed mischief, Isaac, ye never said a truer word. I was mortal angry, but contained mysel'. I thanked her dryly, and said that though the governess had raxed her fit she was still able enough to gie the bairn her lessons."

"Um!—I see through't," said Isaac, delivering the exclamation through his nose.

The gardener was more than usually communicative, and Janet, an earnest student of his demeanour, helped him to a favourite piece of the cheek. Her respect for his perspicacity was unbounded.

" Jenny Guililand," she said, "if you're through wi' your denner rin doon to the candle-maker's and speir for the guidwife's rheumatics — see, gie the dug these banes i' the by-gaun."

It was clear to her Isaac had some idea in his mind that was verified or vivified by Mrs. Cowie's visit, which he might be loath to reveal in the presence of a third party.

" That's prime ! " he exclaimed, leaning back in his chair, and wiping his mouth with open hand after the girl had retired. His colloquist, however, was in dubiety as to whether the adjective referred to the sheep's head or some coincident thought in his own mind.

"Ye have a wonnerfu' head for putting this and that thegither though ye hain yer speech."

"Umph'm — I see her game."

" I'm sure ye see clean through her for a' sic a clever woman as she is." The housekeeper spoke with stimulating emphasis.

"I see her game," Isaac reiterated, not yet ready to capitulate. He was vain of his reticence as garrulous people are of speech.

" I was sure o' that," confirmed Mistress Izet,

"I saw it in your face while I was telling ye what passed."

"I jaloused a while sin," progressed Isaac — "but I never let on."

"Think o' that. Folk that are aye talking seldom learn muckle. Ye think and ken heaps o' things that wud be worth listening to, I'm sure."

"Maybe." The dawn of a grim smile increased while he fingered his lips. "Maybe — but ye should ken this ane — she wants to put her daughter Bell in Miss Hetty's place."

Isaac did not give his authority for this remark, indeed it is doubtful if ever he heard even a hint of Mrs. Cowie's intentions. Probably it was due to the wonderful head he had for putting this and that together. Mrs. Cowie it is true had not at first thought of her daughter going to live at Broomfields in the capacity of a governess, but on after consideration she inquired of herself why not? Bell had got an educational finish which cost "a bonny penny," and it was lost at the farm. Girls as well off as she went out to genteel places; but the prevailing motive in her mind was that of uniting the fortunes of Broomfields and Windy-yett, however that might be brought about. She cleared the point to her own satisfaction that the situation was not one of servility; it was a move in a game of skill. Rumour gave forth that Mr. Congalton was returning with the intention of settling, for a time at least, in Kilspindie. If her daughter got the place of governess she would have opportunities of impressing him with her worth. She would doubtless sit at table with him, and Mrs. Cowie could not believe that any man situated as he was, and living the lonely life he led, could resist a well-favoured young woman like Bell. Mrs. Cowie had looked at the subject out and in. Eva need not be a standing incumbrance. The question was one of generalship. After marriage the child could be sent to a boarding school. That would leave Bell's hands free for the responsibilities that might follow; she felt it would be unfair that a second wife in the early days of her married life should be hampered by the presence and care of a first wife's bairn. Mrs. Cowie was too earnest to see the humour of the situation. She had turned these and kindred matters over in her own mind, but would keep them to herself till the issues were ripe. She felt the tenure of the present governess need not be a long one, indeed so far as her own designs went, she hoped and believed that it would not be so. She passed a condescending "Guid day" to Nancy Beedam and William Caughic, who stood at their respective doors as she sailed down to the inn.

Meantime Windy-yett and his friend the carrier had "yoked" to their second gill. The latter was carried away, and had magnified the incident of the previous afternoon into an act of heroism beyond reasonable proportions. It was an adventure in which he had borne part: there was reflected glory.

"It was smart o' the bit craitur tae," admitted the farmer, thinking of the mere physical aspect of the occurrence, "brocht up on book-diet."

"Book-diet!" repeated McLennan, "man Windy-yett, that's just it." The carrier brought down a solid fist on the table, making the pewter measure gyrate. "It's edication that dis't."

The farmer missed the relevancy of this remark, and asked what "edication" had "to do wi't." He was normally slow in the up-take, but had the reputation at market of being able in the course of the second gill to see as far as his neighbours into a "logic argyment."

"Everything," cried McLennan extravagantly, "at ony rate mair than ye think. Tak your common five-eicht woman, or man either, and spring sudden danger on them, nine oot o' ten o' them'll tak to their heels — self-preservation is the first law wi' them; but here is a lassie, weel brocht up, weel schuled, wi' her wits under control. Her training has gi'en her the whip-hand o' hersel', so to speak. Man, she didna even squeal, and that showed edication. She had been taught to think o' ithers before hersel', and crying oot couldna work a miracle. It wud have been a waste o' breath, and she needed a' her puff to rin to the dyke and drap the wee thing safe on the ither side. D'ye see?" The carrier was getting into form. "It's the same thing i' the British army — the rank and file will stick and kill stracht-foret like deevils, but what wud come o't if this bruit-force wasna under the guidance o' a calm mind? It's the

officers that win the battles. Man, edication
will —— "

But what more this wonderful agency was
capable of achieving, according to the appraisement of this advocate whom it had neglected,
remained unexpressed, for Mrs. Cowie had
thrown the door back forcibly to the wall, and
stood in the opening. She was annoyed at the
impatient and curt treatment received at the
hands of Mistress Izet, but the annoyance developed into wrath on finding that her husband had
not only forgotten her, but had so far forgotten
himself as to consort with and treat a common
carrier for the purpose of hearing about the
" silly on-gauns o' a glaikit woman." This was
what she said afterwards, but at the moment she
stood in the door, an alarming embodiment of
impatience, and only remarked, " Are you
ready? I'm waiting for ye."

As her husband in unheroic haste " clamped "
past to the stable the carrier asked politely
if he could treat her to a " gless o' sherry
wine."

" No, thenk ye," she said, raising her chin.
" I'm much obleeged to ye, but I dinna approve

o' women or men either drinking in a common change-hoose on the Sabbath day." She turned on her heel and metaphorically shook the dust of connivance from her feet.

Cowie held the horse's head meekly until she was solidly settled in the gig, then he mounted beside her and drove up the brae, bracing himself for what might ensue. They passed Broomfields in silence. The dram and the carrier's words were still buzzing in Richard Cowie's head. His wife's eyes were turned away from him as if she were studying nature amongst the weeds and wild flowers at the roots of the hedge. He felt that his forgetfulness had given her "mortal" offence. In ordinary circumstances he would have waited humbly and let her have her say, but his share of two gills hadn't been taken for nothing; he would have the first word, let who might have the last. He sucked his tongue encouragingly to the horse and applied the whip.

"I agree wi' McLennan that edication's a gran' thing," he began, as if his wife had been a listener to their interrupted discussion.

" D'ye though," she retorted, shifting her eyes

from the hedge-roots. "It's a pity but ye baith had mair o' t."

His valour was rising.

"Tak ony ither common lassie," he continued, "ten to ane wud 'a' ta'en to their heels and ran withoot thinking o' the bit bairn; but that's whare edication comes in. It's the same with the British army, the men will rin ram-stam and stick this ane and the ither ane, but it's the offishers that wins the battles."

His wife turned to him at first with concern, then a withering look contorted her face.

"The whisky has gane to yer head," she said.

"Na, it's sober truth, McLennan and me had a prime crack aboot it. He saw the governess rinnin' wi' the wee lassie in her arms and the bull at her heels. He puts it a' doon to edication, and I'm inclined to favour his opinion. They tell me the woman got badly hurt hersel', did ye hear ocht c't?"

Richard Cowie's audacity had surprised even himself. He did not know his wife's designs, if she had confided in him probably he would not have gone so far.

"Ay," she remarked dryly, "so you're agreed that edication's a gran' thing, baith o' ye, and that the British army wins battles by it; weel, weel, yer an uncommon pair, but ony subject will serve men when there's whisky i' their insides."

"Ye needna flyte, it didna cost that muckle siller," he said humbly.

"Ay, ay; it's the cock's guidwill wi' the hen's corn, but it wud have been a heap wicer-like gin ye had been talking owre the heads o' the day's discoorse, than exposing the silly on-gauns o' a glaikit woman in a public change-hoose."

Windy-yett began to consider as he drove along that he had somehow started on the wrong "headrigg." He certainly had the first word, and it might be as well he thought now to let his wife have the last, because it came to his memory that there was another subject that had to be broached with pacific carefulness before he reached home. During the day, while cracking thoughtlessly in the kirkyard, he had taken the liberty of inviting Willie Mitchell of Coultarmains to dinner. This hospitable impulse had come into his mind on learning that the young farmer's sister-housekeeper had gone to visit a friend at Kingsford, and would not return till the Monday.

"I'm fell sorry I keepit ye waiting," he said by and by, in a preparatory way. "Edication efter a's no everything, though McLennan was gey dour on't." He was nearing the road-end, and he did not want Willie Mitchell to feel that he, Richard Cowie, had no standing in his own house. "I forgot to tell ye I had speired Coultarmains to denner the day." He had reined the pony to walking pace, and was mopping his head with a red pocket-handkerchief.

"Ye what?" cried his wife, almost bouncing off her seat, and stamping her foot with a force that to his innocent mind seemed out of all proportion to his indiscretion. But the look of vexation and anger on her face was even more alarming than her words or gestures.

Willie Mitchell invited to dinner! Were her plans and cherished hopes to be frustrated by the stupid intermeddling of a thoughtless man? This was the secret of Bell's absence; the reason of her desire to walk instead of drive home. Mrs. Cowie was not so insensible to the language of look and manner as to be ignorant of the fact that the "Mains" lad had a fancy for Bell, and that her daughter, like a wayward, unsought girl, was none loath to receive his attentions. The farm of Coultarmains had been left to Mitchell and his sister, well-stocked, and free of debt; but for Bell, with her ladylike accomplishments, to go into a farm kitchen possessing simply a third partnership, with probably two to one against her, would be a folly which must be hindered. But beyond and above this, such a union would blight all her maternal ambitions, and involve the sacrifice of her interest in the doctor's will. These considerations flashed through Mrs. Cowie's mind in a moment, and emphasized the terrible peremptoriness of word and manner.

"Weel, ye see, I had no chance o' speirin ye i' the kirk," Cowie said deferentially, "for the precentor was half through the first psalm before I won up to the laft, and efter we were oot this meeserable governess story dang the thing clean oot o' my head."

"Sin' ye have invited Mains yoursel', ye maun een have him to yersel'; as for me and Bell, we'll denner i' the kitchen."

" Ye'll no do ony sic an onnecbourly thing, surely," he said pleadingly. " His sister has gane to Kingsford, and as there was to be no set-doon denner for him at hame, I thought ye wudna mind me asking him to tak a bite wi' us o' what was gaun."

His wife did not reply. They had turned up the loaning leading to the farm, and she had need of the short space of time remaining to make up her mind. As they drove into the court she saw Bell with a pink rose in her hand sitting at one side of the parlour window, chatting gaily with a brown-faced, soft-eyed young far-mer, who sat at the other. By the momentary glance inward she saw Bell had spread the damask table-cloth and put down the "company" knives and forks. It is not wronging her to say that Mrs. Cowie was pleased with Bell's fore-thought. She felt it was proper to impress this young man with their genteel manners, because their very " style " would show him how hopeless any matrimonial pretensions on his part would prove. She would not lower herself in the esteem of a neighbour by adhering to the inhospitable threat she had flung at her husband,

89

but she would take care that he had no chance of palavering privately with Bell. The embarrassment of the moment had also shown her the time had come when it was necessary that both her husband and Bell should understand her wishes, so that no family cross-purpose in future should interfere with the realization of her plans.

CHAPTER VIII

THE PRODIGAL'S RETURN

" Eva, Eva, come fast and help me to catch
this beautiful creature."

There was a rapid rustle of skirts in and
out among the broom and boulders, quickening
breath, and at last rippling palpitations of
laughter as the pursuers dropped exhausted
on a thymey knoll under the gracious shadow
of a clump of hazels.

" I did not know pansies could fly," Eva
said, with round eyes, when her breath had
returned. " Oh, Miss Hetty, you had it in
your parasol."

Hetty laughed at the dainty conceit.

" It was not a pansy, dear, but a lovely
butterfly; see, there it is again, hovering above
that wild rose bush, but it is safe, for we cannot
follow it over the burn."

The governess and her companion were on their way to the Baidland Cairn. Their sensations of pleasure in the warm and fragrant air were enhanced by contrast. The previous afternoon was chill and leaden, slashed with grey lines of windy rain. From the school-room window Eva watched the distant trees tossing wispy tops of sombre green, while occasionally she turned a pink imaginative ear to the garden to catch the answer the flowers were whispering back to the rain. But this dreary, disappointing afternoon was succeeded by a perfect day, led in by the lark, and perfumed by the sweet odours of wood and corn-land. To Eva it brought the additional pleasure of a letter from her father, informing her that his book was out, and that he was leaving London the day after he wrote, and hoped to be back at Broomfields by the end of the week. Surely an early release from lessons and a long invigorating romp on the wholesome hillsides was not an unearned relaxation on such a day. They left the shade of the hazels, and were ascending the fern-fringed path, when the towsy head of a boy suddenly appeared above the dry stone dyke on their right. He held a young turnip by the green tops in one hand, and a piece of white unenveloped paper in the other. The turnip was soft and succulent, and bore marks of strong appreciative teeth — it was not to be parted with, but he held out the paper to Hetty.

"I'm hurdin," he explained, "and canna come owre. If the kye miss me they'll be in the neeps."

Hetty went over to the dyke.

"What is it?" she inquired, taking the proffered paper from the boy's hand.

"I canna read it," he replied honestly. "It's frae a gangrel. I was to wait for an answer."

Eva looked at the ragged apparition with puzzled, wondering gaze; but the apparition went on munching his turnip with light-hearted unconcern. Then the gleam of a generous thought came over his face and his grey eyes softened.

"Tak' a bite," he said, holding the juicy end of the turnip out to Eva; "it's an awfu' sweet ane."

What did this strange missive say, the reading of which touched the full gamut of Hetty's sensations as she stood there, pale and red, cold and hot by turns, totally oblivious to what was passing around her? This is what it said —

"Dear Hetty, I have just got your address; but although I am so near you my rig-out is not respectable enough for me to call at your place, or appear before you in the light of day. If you watch the boy returning you will see I am waiting your reply in the neighbourhood of the cross-roads. Could you meet me there at dusk? No one knows I have come back; much depends on seeing you alone. Just say yes or no to the boy. If you cannot come to-night I will wait at Drumoyne inn till I hear from you."

"You poor hungry little boy," Eva was saying; "have you nothing good to eat at home?"

Hetty folded the paper and laughingly explained to her pupil what a delicious thing to a boy a fresh young turnip is. Then she put a small silver coin in the messenger's hand.

"For him?" he inquired, pointing with the remainder of the turnip over his shoulder.

" No, for yourself."

The boy's eyes beamed incredulously.

" And what for the gangrel?"

" Just say — Yes."

The boy flung away the end of the turnip and took to his heels. For a brief space there was the rapid twinkling of two short legs, bare to the knees, over the swelling bosom of the clover field, then gradually feet, legs, body and head, the latter still wagging, seemed to sink into the ground as the eyes of the watchers passed on to the golden shimmer of the wheat-land in the hollow beyond. Eva was too much engrossed with this child of the soil to observe her companion's discomposure.

The letter was from her cousin, Willie Hazlet, who had been a source of trouble to his relations. It was the old story, and not without parallel in the experience of many families. A well-intentioned attempt had been made to elevate the boy beyond his natural station, to lift him by education and association into a position which he had not the moral capacity to appreciate or retain. His father, in placing him in a high-class school, endeavoured frankly to impress upon him that he was paying beyond his means, and warned him against indulging in the belief that he could afterwards be maintained on the same social plane. These admonitions entered the boy's ear, but they did not influence his reason. He became dissatisfied. To his mind there seemed to be something wrong in the economy of things. Why should *his* father not have plenty of money like the fathers of other boys? Somehow he got it into his head that it was parsimoniousness, and not actual want of substance, that was at the bottom of his own lack of liberal pocket-money, and the lectures on thrift to which he was subjected both in correspondence and during his vacation holidays. At the age of eighteen he was removed from school; the restraints of home-life were irksome. He wanted freedom and money to spend. Many of the fellows got leave to travel abroad with a tutor or companion. He wished to see life as other fellows saw it, not in the restricted circle of a provincial town, but in a grander sphere, where there was breadth and freedom. The expensive education had proved a double failure; it had left him dissatisfied, as well as insufficiently qualified to enter even on the preliminary stages of a professional career. A junior clerkship in a bank occupied him for a time, but this, after numerous and vexatious episodes, he left, and clandestinely betook himself to sea. Hetty was pleased to hear from the wayward, self-willed prodigal, about whose fate they had feared the worst. She remembered him as a bright-faced, kind-hearted, and impulsive boy, when he used to spend his school holidays at the manse. The present might be the turning-point in his life. He had appealed to her, and she felt it to be her duty to respond to the appeal.

Hetty and her pupil continued their stroll to the top of the Baidlands, where they rested in the breezy sunshine, overlooking the undulating strath, through which the silver cord of the Garnet meandered, leading the eye onward past tawny cornfields to a sombre belt of pines, behind which the hazy smoke of Drumoyne, sheltered by the hill, curled and climbed. The one was thinking of the chequered wanderings of a wayward sailor lad, while the other speculated audibly as to the presents her father would bring from London, and whether he would remain at home and never go away any more.

The upper disc of the sun was level with the tree-tops in Crosby Glen, and the reflected glow illumined the Manse windows as Hetty set out to keep her tryst. On nearing the spot where the main thoroughfare intersects the parish road she paused to still her pulse — eagerness had unconsciously given nimbleness to her step. There was a man on the slope of the parish road; a woman was approaching him from the opposite direction; for a moment they paused and spoke. The quick, searching eye of the sailor caught sight of his cousin as she emerged from the shadow of the hedge. As they saluted each other the figure on the hill paused, her back against the after-glow, and witnessed their meeting. The young man was the first to speak.

" I must begin our interview with an apology," he said. " It was too bad my asking you to meet me in this way, but I wanted your advice, Hetty, and could not appear in this garb at any respectable door." His weather-worn, tar-stained clothes were not at variance with his words.

"Do not trouble about that," she replied. "I am so glad to see you home. How did you know where to find me? I was pleased to get your message."

"I ran away from the ship at Greenock, and of course forfeited my wages. I am sick of this life, but dare not go back to my father. I came to Drumoyne thinking to go on to the manse at Kilbaan, but learned from the innkeeper what changes had taken place there. Hetty, I have been a fool. I feel I am unworthy to look in any of your faces again."

"You need not speak like that, Willie; indeed you must not." The girl was moved by the bitter tone of self-reproach. "Your father is still your father, though you have not behaved well to him."

"Oh, I dare not expect anything from that quarter," he said rather cynically. "He wrote me after I left that as I had disregarded all his counsels, and so on; you know the kind of thing. My father has always been very severe."

"Do not be unreasonable, Willie; you admit

that your conduct has been foolish, and your father's severity, as you call it, was all meant in kindness to correct your faults. But how can I help you? After all that has taken place, I think it is your duty to write home and ask forgiveness."

" And be told that having made a thorny bed I must lie on it."

" No, Willie, I am sure you do your father injustice. If you are really sorry for your past, and say so to him frankly, I believe he would give you a fresh start. But was not this your own desire when you wrote me? What do you propose yourself?"

" I can hardly tell," he replied honestly, betraying the frailty of an irresolute mind. " I half thought of the army. Do you think I could get on as a soldier?"

His cousin looked in his downcast, helpless face. There was no strength of purpose in it. The army, she was sure, was a new fad, which would soon become as distasteful to him as the sea. It was another folly.

" No," she replied resolutely; " I do not think you would get on as a soldier. You do not

know what such a life means. Besides, it would
be too late to change your mind when you
discovered you did not like it. You tire of
the sea, and the only penalty you pay for
leaving it is the forfeiture of your wages; but
you could not thus get away from the army.
You doubt your father's forgiveness — I do not.
Try which of us is right. If your belief should
prove true, then the army is open to you.
Willie," she said, taking the lad by the hand,
her kindly eyes looking straight into his, " I
think too much of you to let you go further
wrong. You have invited me here to advise
you — will you take my advice?"

He turned his face away from her gaze.
There were tears in his voice as he spoke.

" Hetty," he said, " I believe you are right;
but — but I cannot — just yet. I feel —— "

" I know what you are thinking," she interrupted; " you cannot go back as you are. That
can be put right. See, here is my purse." She
had thought of this before leaving home, and
put all her savings in it. " You will pay me
back when you can. Put away your sea-clothes
and get others. Go straight to Kilbaan; I will

write to my sister — she will expect you. I am sure also my father will write and make reconciliation easy. Trust on your father's part may be slow of coming — it can only be entirely established, after what has taken place, by honourable and persevering work. Are you prepared for that?"

"I will do my very best, Hetty," he said, with decision, the dawn of an honest purpose appearing on his face. "Then the result I anticipate is sure to follow." There was new resolution in his hand-shake at parting as he kissed her brow.

Hetty stood till his figure was silhouetted from the apex of the hill against the lingering rose of sunset. Poor boy! what a long race he had taken from his father's house to learn the comforts of home.

As she turned homeward there was a crackling amongst the brushwood behind the beech hedge. It was probably a sheep, or a delinquent collie among the rabbits. Joy shut the door against fear; her cousin Willie was dead, but was now alive again. She would hurry home and write the heartening news to Violet.

CHAPTER IX

A ROUP AT SMIDDY-YARD

THERE was a displenishing sale at Smiddy-yard — a roup it was called — and all the country-side turned out to buy, or see how prices ranged. Smiddy-yard was a large, well-stocked hill farm, owned by the late Stephen Barbour, better known as the Rev. Steenie Barbour, owing to his habitual use of scriptural forms of speech. In early life he was three parts on for the ministry, but "reisted" at fore-ordination and free will. He turned his college-lear to farming in succession to his father, and prospered. Two sons, inheriting their father's tastes, were at college, and the widow, being well left, resolved to displenish the farm and remove with her boys to the city.

The farm steading was large, and included a superior dwelling-house, barn, byre, stable, hay-loft, and potato-sheds, with an expansive court-yard between. Round about the walls of the outhouses all manner of implements — ploughs, harrows, carts, churns, a dog-cart, cheese-presses, a winnowing machine, flails, and such like — were arranged in the order of convenience, and numbered for the purpose of sale. In the milk house a table was plenished with various eatables — home-made scones, oatcakes, loaves of white-bread, and milk. There was also a couple of small casks of ale laid on trestles. This provision on the face of it betokened hospitable welcome to neighbours, but if frankness be allowed, it was also designed to promote business and hinder adjournment elsewhere; while inside, in the best parlour, liquids and solids of a more genteel order were provided for family friends possessing palates of subtler culture. There was little work done that day for five miles around, for even farm servants who had not permission to leave home, feeling the yoke easy in their master's absence, kept on dreaming about the humours of the occasion, the wholesome fare of which they were not allowed to be partakers, and idled their hours away over reminiscences of roups at which they themselves had been present.

The inquisitive rooks in the Garnet woods came out again and circled above Kilspindie wondering, for no anvil rang, and not a shuttle was thrown. The tinsmith deserted his soldering iron, the candle-maker suspended his frame, and let the tallow cool. Even McLennan left the road for a day, and entrusted Brownie and the cart to his brother-in-law, the dry-stone dyker, and mingled in the human tide that impinged on Smiddy-yard. By ten o'clock the field behind the farm was littered with all kinds of conveyances. Horses, freed from their trappings, and others wearing odd articles of harness, browsed contentedly among the cool succulent grass. Windy-yett and his wife were amongst the earliest arrivals. His desires were bounded by the thought of a cheap, serviceable horse; hers had a wider horizon and a weightier purpose, which for the present it was her own business to conceal. It was a motley gathering that found its way to the hillside farm on that fresh, early autumn morning. Responsible landowners, bonnet-lairds, farmers, otherwise a nondescript crowd, leavened and toned by the controlling presence of Mr. Maconkey the parish minister. The less valuable articles were disposed of first to give voice to the bidders, and allow time for important arrivals. The auctioneer was a man of encouraging humour. Natural tact and long experience had taught him how to handle the materials of a roup, and stir the cupidity of buyers. The sacrifice of a few comparatively worthless things to begin with would excite expectation, and prepare the unwary mind for bargains. A couple of " stoups " and a watering-can were recklessly thrown away to Babby Lawson. Tinny Walker became the possessor of an anvil. The carrier enhanced his own professional usefulness by the acquisition of a hand-barrow, and Ritchie Meiklem, plough-man at the mains, had a cradle knocked down to him amidst the plaudits of the company. This was acknowledged to be a providence of forethought, inasmuch as Ritchie had only been "cried" (proclaimed in church) for the second time on the previous Sunday. But the ploughman heroically faced the merriment by saying, "a roup didna happen every day."

When they had time to encompass its import

the women-folk were sore scandalized. Mrs. Caughie rubbed her knotted knuckles, and whispered severely to Nancy Beedam that it was "an unco ondecent like thing," while Pringle the smith slapped the now blushing purchaser on the back —

"There is nothing like lookin' foret, lad," he said; "gin ye dinna need it yersel', ye'll fin' folk'll gie your ain siller for 't."

The cartwright's humour became illustrative.

"What the smith says is richt, Ritchie," he said, taking the ploughman aside; "aye have odds and ends handy. Ye'll maybe mind John Halliday, him that got the place in the Glasgow bank; weel, things fell oot wi' the mistress rather afore-han', and I'm told he was seen wan night efter the darkning driving aboot in a cab seekin' for safety preens."

About mid-day most of the miscellaneous articles outside were disposed of, and half-an-hour's adjournment was allowed for refreshments. Windy-yett had lost his wife in the crowd, or rather she had deserted him for her own ends, and feeling for the moment a free hand, he retired with the smith to the dairy to

have a " bite o' something to eat, and a wacht
o' yill." General Alexander had just arrived
from Blacklaw, and it was known he had a mind
to purchase a couple of young horses for car-
riage-work : the " horse beasts " were to be
taken first on the resumption of business. The
promiscuous discourse in the dairy was outspoken and hilarious, neighbour chaffing or congratulating neighbour over their purchases.
Brinkburn had got " a michty bargain " of the
winnowing machine. A plough and a couple
of harrows had gone to Meilkeflat for the price
" o' auld airn ; " while there had been a " keen
toozzle " between Coultarmains and Auchentorlie
over a dog-cart, that had fallen to the latter at
a price which the cartwright — being a practical
man — declared for extravagance was " clean oot
o't." Cowie had a mind only for one thing
at a time, and preferred the prospective to
the backward look. He was concerned about
how prices might go when the sale resumed.
As was the custom, he knew the less costly
beasts would go first. In this class might be
reckoned the working-horse which under the
dominant influence of a superior will he had

been inspired to purchase. "Dinna miss it for
the sake o' a bid," was the latest utterance of
the superior will, giving latitude. "Bess is owre
licht for field work: noo that Bell is an heiress
she maun gang aboot, and Bess will be braw
and serviceable i' the gig." Cowie, feeling the
"yill," and fearing indiscretion, went in search
of his wife.

Meantime the object of quest was seated in the
best parlour, in absorbing confabulation with Mrs.
Lonen, the school-master's wife, when the conversation was interrupted by General Alexander,
who, out of gallant consideration for the ladies'
needs, asked them what refreshment they would
have. Mrs. Cowie, who "was carrying forward
the crack," impressively looked up a little
flustered. Then she smiled graciously — "it was
sic an honour to be waited on by a high-born
gentleman."

"I had a real herty breakfast thenk you,"
she said, wishing it to be understood that the
notion of eating and drinking at the cost of
Smiddy-yard could not be entertained without
pressure. The General replied affably that he
could recommend the sherry, and as for the

sandwiches, they were excellent — it was long since breakfast time. With just sufficient hesitation to justify apparent indifference, and make compliance lady-like, she said —

"Weel, General, since you are so very kind, I'll tak' a gless o' sherry wine and a sangwidge."

From her advanced "pronouncemanship," as she called it, of uncommon words, she would show the General they were not foreign to her. The school-master's wife, though eager for news, was conscious of human needs which she was none loath to gratify. After the episode of refreshment, the women settled down again with their heads together to the unfinished crack.

"Really, Mrs. Cowie, ye surprise me. A common sailor, did ye say?"

"Ay, 'deed, a common sailor, and a strong, ill-set looking tyke too. I was just coming back i' the gloaming from my sister's at Crosby, when I saw him sauntering aboot the road en' downright suspicious like. I thocht my gentleman had tint his gate, or maybe he was efter some uncanny ploy, so I made bold to speak, but he was barely ceevil, and lurched past me.

It was on looking over my shoulder that I got a glint o' her coming up the loaning."

" There would be a tryst — like enough."

" Oh, they didna meet there by chance, ye may rely on that, Mrs. Lonen, and from what I saw and heard efter-hin', I feel there was mair than friendliness atween them."

" Eh, the cunning piece — weel, woman?"

" Mrs. Lonen, what do ye think I did? I'm no one bit ashamed to tell ye, though ye ken I'm the last woman that would pry into ither folk's ongauns; but when I thought o' the late Dr. Congalton's niece, a puir, innocent, un-suspectin' bairn left to the care o' a woman that could steal oot i' the darkenin' to meet a man that, for a' I kent, might be a common keelie (thief) or a cut-throat, I stepped across the field into the wood, and was behind the beech hedge or ever they won to the ither side o't. They spoke low, and I didna just catch a' that passed, but she spoke maist, and seemed to be pleading wi' him. Mrs. Lonen, ye have seen a heap o' the world, and I need not mint my suspicions to you, but ye ken brawly there's aye something wrang when a woman steals oot secretly under cover o' night to plead wi' a man!"

There was a pause, to let the remark gather importance.

" I couldna see their faces, but I think or a' was dune she was in tears: — then he kissed her. I heard it! Yes, Mrs. Lonen, the shameless hussy actually stood up and let the man kiss her i' the open road. That's the wye o' yer fine governess gentry. The parish schule wasna guid enough for the bit bairn, but my certie, Mr. Congalton made a sair mistake when he put his daughter under a woman like yon."

" But Janet Izet should ken, or Isaac Kilgour, they wud speak to the maister."

" It's no use — they're baith clean glamourt, and 'll no hear a word against her. Noo that Mr. Congalton's back somebody maun tell, of course, but it's a story no modest woman can mint to a strange man."

" We could speak to the minister," whispered Mrs. Lonen, nudging her friend. The individual spoken of was sipping whisky and water humanly enough at the other side of the table.

Mrs. Cowie shook her head — this was not in
the drift of her intention, but she endeavoured
to justify her negation.

"The minister and her father are said to be
auld frien's — class-mates i' the college, or something o' the kind ; but mair than that, from
what I've heard tell, Mr. Congalton has but
little faith in ministers. No, Mrs. Lonen, the
thing wud come wi' far greater force from your
ain guidman. They tell me the twa were real
chief before Mr. Congalton gaed to London ;
and no to be wondered at either, baith being
book-learned and leeterary."

The school-master's wife proudly admitted
that Mr. Congalton had occasionally smoked
a pipe before leaving for London at the school-
house — indeed one of the first things he had
done on his return the previous day, was to
call and present a copy of his new book to her
husband.

" Ye see that," and Mrs. Cowie's face beamed ;
" nothing could be better — nothing could be
more providential, as I might say. The men
smoking their pipes and cracking owre the
news ; the thing will come up as natural as
8   113

ye like. I'm willing to tell a' I ken at the right time, however painfu' it may be, but, Mrs. Lonen, it maun be real private, ye ken, and he maun speir."

Windy-yett had for some time been standing at the parlour door cap in hand, trying ineffectually to attract his wife's attention. Mrs. Lonen was the first to catch sight of him, and having promised to mention the matter to her husband, the farmer's wife, satisfied that the leaven would work, bustled out of the room.

" Save us guidwife, ye're among gentry the day ! " said Windy-yett, rendered jocose by the self-complacent glow on his partner's face.

" Ay, among the gentry no less," she replied, " wi' a General to serve 's too ; but I've tell't my story to that body Mrs. Lonen, and there'll be few in Kilspindie that'll no hear't or the day's dune."

The farmer was wishful that his wife should stand by and prompt him at the bidding, in order, as he said, that there might be " no back-spangs." The basis of their mutual understanding, moreover, had been slightly disturbed by the information he had received from the

smith. The understanding was as to the probable price at which the horse might go. He
had learned that the beast had received an
injury, and was now a "roarer."

"Then it should go a five-pound-note
cheaper, at the very least," Mrs. Cowie remarked. "Gavin Lindsay, the innkeeper at
Dalwhinzie, I am told, wants the horse for gig
use, and may bid against ye; but dinna fail
to let him hear it's a roarer. The creature, I'm
told, is a willing beast, and would serve us weel
enough for leisurely work. A dram'll no be
lost on Pringle gin ye get him to gi'e the horse
a guid race before the bidding begins."

Windy-yett, armed by his wife's authority
to give and take refreshment after the purchase,
sought the smith and confided his plan to him.

"Wants it for the gig, does he?" said the
latter with a significant nod, then he took the
halter from the stable-boy, slapped the creature
on the flank, and set off at a violent pace down
the field. When he returned Gavin Lindsay
seemed to have his mouth buttoned at both
ends, and Wattie Dron, the cadger from Kil-
mallie, who aspired to a horse, got to the end

of his means by one opposition bid, so that the roarer fell to Cowie considerably under its intrinsic value as a serviceable horse.

Windy-yett and his friend waited till General Alexander had made his purchase, which was completed after brisk competition between himself and the factor, then they retired to the Railway inn for the well-earned dram.

Meantime the assistant auctioneer had just disposed of the contents of one of the rooms inside, and Effie Dougan, in company with Elspeth Marshall, was leaving the house laughing and chatting over the incidents of the sale.

"Cock her up," said the latter, "the siller has turned that woman's head, I'm thinking; a farmer's wife going for to buy an article like thon."

"Eh, she was clean set on 't," responded Mistress Dougan, " and was oot and in the room a' day like a peeweet watchin' its nest. But wasna the ither a funny bit — 'Mrs. Cowie, you're bidding again' yoursel',' says the unc- tioneer. ' Is it mine yet? ' says she, in an unco pliskie. 'No,' says he, and she noddet her

head again." The two gossips passed on
laughing.

When Cowie returned from the inn he found
his wife packing some crockery in the boot
of the dog-cart. She had heard from Coultarmains what her husband had paid for the horse,
and this, combined with her own purchases,
had produced a flush of pleasure and a feeling
of uncommon amiability.

"Ye'll no guess what I've bought," she said,
inviting inquiry after they had yoked, and were
on their way out of the thick of the home-going
vehicles.

"I saw ye putting past some delf," he said,
thinking only of how he and the smith had
managed the purchase of the horse.

"Na, that was nothing but some coorse
crockery-gear for Nance to break, it's something
that'll surprise ye. I bought the Smiddy-yard
book-case."

"What, yon great press wi' the gless doors?"

"Ay," she answered, with defiant good-
nature, " the book-case and the books. I have
the key in my purse. What d'ye think o'
that!"

"Lord save us!" He let the whip-lash fall about Bess' ears in a way that made her think she was expected to break into a gallop, "Wo, then, woa, lass. Are ye gaun to let books oot at so much a week?"

"Na, na," she replied, "it's pairt o' my plans. I got the thing cheap wi' Bell's siller, and of course it will gang wi' Bell. Mr. Congalton is a great writer himsel', and I'm sure he'll no think onything the less o' her for having a guid leebrary o' books."

CHAPTER X

ISAAC KILGOUR COGITATES

THE scene of Isaac Kilgour's daily occupation was enclosed on three sides by hedges of thorn and privet, and on the fourth by a rubble wall, exposed to the southern sun. The wall was veined with healthful shiny branches, amongst which various fruits ripened under fostering leaves. There was a rockery in the centre of the enclosure, surrounded by a moat or trench, in which flowed constantly a crystal purl of cool spring water. On this point the walks converged, sloping downward. It was a garden of the old-fashioned type, containing gnarled bushes with red globes and pendant clusters of fruit, pots where celery blanched, solid lines of peas, cabbages, leeks, green kale, and such other vegetable varieties as could be turned to useful account at any season of the year by a thrifty house-wife in the exercise of her culinary duties. There were flower-beds and borders with roses in abundance, wallflowers whose blooms were now shed, phloxes, and other perennial plants that gave little trouble. So far as the soil was concerned, there was nothing to hinder abundant blossoming and fruiting for, as its late owner used to say, " If ye are kind to the grun' the grun' will be kind to you," and he treated his garden on this principle. Yet this enclosure, with all its natural powers of production, had one draw-back — it was infested with moles. Now if there was any mundane thing that Isaac Kilgour hated more than another it was moles. The eruptive disturbance by these cident creatures of care-fully prepared seed-beds, when labour and ex-pectation were coming to fruition, was enough to ruffle a more philosophic mind than Isaac Kilgour's. He had tried traps, but the cunning "yearthly deevils " had learned to give them the go-bye. Isaac, however, was a dogged man when thwarted. There was another method recently adopted by him in dealing with these subterranean enemies which had proved more effective in their destruction. He bought a narrow trenching spade which the smith had ground and set to the keenness of a knife-blade. With this implement he would steal out on the early summer and autumn mornings in felt slippers, and taking his stand where he could see the first quiverings of the soil, he would move noiselessly to the spot, and strike with remorseless aim into the loose earth. Isaac had attained remarkable skill in these operations, and his spade was seldom unearthed without sanguinary evidence that the enemy had suffered. He had some of the instincts of a true sportsman, and the pleasure of slaughter in this special direction had grown into a passion like fishing or shooting. The thought of it drew him early from bed. At times he would bring forth the parrot and hang the cage on some sunny spot where the inquisitive, ever-observant eye of the bird could see. "Clip the moudie, clip the moudie," it would cry encouragingly, as it watched the gardener moving cat-like to the scene of action. Then when the blow was struck it would chuckle a strange guttural laugh, and commence in a high-toned, fairly soft voice to sing what might have been the post-mortem reflections of the mole — "Up in the morning's no for me, up in the morning ear—ley."

It was a blue, cloudless morning; such perfume-bearing roses as the garden possessed were past, but there was the scent of old-fashioned carnations and southernwood in the dewy air. The comings and goings of footsteps were visible in the grass where lines of dullness marred the diamond glitter of the dew. Isaac had already struck his spade with mortal directness six times into the rising soil. He paused to wipe the perspiration from under his cap, for there was excitement in this occupation which aided the physical exercise in giving pace to his not over active blood. The morning was too far advanced for such pastime, even although there had been moles left to tempt further mortality. The parrot had witnessed the activity of its master, and was in a flutter of garrulous excitement. Many new phrases had got into its mimic head, caught up from Eva and the governess, whose tones, as well as words, it could reproduce with remarkable accuracy. Isaac sat down on a block of wood under an umbrageous maple, and lighting his half-filled short clay pipe, let the creature talk.

" Pretty Poll, pretty Poll — ey — clever bird — O — you bee—uty," it went on; occasionally lapsing into the vernacular, " Eh, haud yer tongue — irr ye there? — there's Janet."

Isaac sat looking dreamily at the rockery without seeing it. He was the last of his family. Old Tam Kilgour, his father, had been, to Isaac's shame, the latest survivor. He was a notorious poacher, and too fond of a dram; even other-wise he had not been a good man. Perhaps the best that could be said of him was said by Willie Faill, when he and others had been invited to see him before being " nailed doon." " Weel, weel," Willie said, scratching his head in a swither, "there lies Tam Kilgour; whatever waggin tongues might say aboot him when in life, he maks a real decent corp." Isaac had no near relatives alive that he could trace. He had been brought up in Mauchline, where in youth he was engaged as a stable-boy. Later he was trans-ferred to Kilspindie to drive Dr. Congalton's carriage, and fill up his spare time in the garden. He and Mistress Izet had grown old together in the same service. She was his junior by perhaps five years. In early life she had a fair dower of comeliness, to which Isaac was not insensible. It could not be said he courted her — he was rather shy for that. The young housekeeper, however, was too human to keep him altogether out of her thoughts. Probably if things had been left alone, mutual regard might have come to the fruition of matrimony. Zedie Lawson's wife was the unintentional means of putting an end to her sister's prospects in this direction. She was a presumptuous, masterful woman, but her force of character had no feminine delicacy in it. Unknown to her sister she sent for Isaac, and said bluntly to him she thought it was high time he was marrying Janet. From that moment the spell under which the young couple were insensibly creeping was broken. Janet Izet was distressed at the unwisdom, not to say immodesty, of her sister's interference; and Isaac's shyness and Janet's sense of shame took such a severe form of self-consciousness, that for many a day they never spoke to each other, unless compelled to do so by the call of duty. Out of this period of constraint they emerged in the course of years, but it was as if they had been born again in the relationship of brother and sister. They were cognisant of each other's weaknesses, about which they spoke freely, and each other's good qualities, but of these they had no mutual converse at all.

The leaf shadows were fluttering like lark-wings on the garden walk while Isaac smoked. Physically he was exhausted with his morning's work — or sport, for it had the elements of both.

"The moudies are by for the day," he said, speaking vaguely in the air, but it had not been of the "moudies" he was thinking during the last ten minutes of reflective idleness. "There's Janet," screamed the bird at his side, and then it sent out a metallic peal of cackling laughter, as its master turned his head involuntarily toward the kitchen door, for it was indeed of her he had been idly dreaming during his reverie. The night before Mistress Izet and Isaac had been summoned into Mr. Congalton's study, where he supplemented his knowledge of the history of their connection with the house by personal inquiry. He told them it was his present intention

to remain at Kilspindie for a time, but that circumstances might occur to call him away at once,
either for a considerable period or permanently.
Should the latter event take place — and it was
not unlikely — he would arrange, in virtue of their
long service to his brother, that such provision
should be made as would help to keep them
from want during the remainder of their lives.
It was his wish that in the meantime they
should continue their duties under him as they
had done under his late brother, but he thought
it due to them, as old and faithful servants, to
make them aware of his intentions, that they
might be in no perplexity about the future.

Isaac had retired to his castle of one apartment
as if it had been a baronial residence. Indeed
the assurance of being preserved from actual
want was to him more than a superfluity of
wealth, for, as he thought in his own mind,
money beyond what is requisite to satisfy one's
personal needs as often as not brings the reverse
of happiness. During the watches of the night
he had rolled this sweet morsel of intelligence
under a metaphorical tongue. It was so com-
forting to possess a secure sense of immediate

independence. Under its stimulus he had risen early and killed six moles. But as the day advanced the mental horizon had widened and let in other considerations. For over thirty years he had gone in and out of Broomfields finding his simple prayer for daily bread answered with unfailing regularity. Breakfast at eight, dinner at twelve, tea at five, and brose before going to bed, barring the interference of professional irregularities, but even when these infrequent exigencies intervened something hot and toothsome was always forthcoming by the time he got the mare stabled and fed. Such washing, dressing, and mending as he required were done so unobtrusively that he almost forgot he had this blessing also to be thankful for. Now and again he was partially awakened to the consideration of what was being done for him by the remark—"Ye'll gang on wearing thae flannens till they'll no wash white," or, "Ye maun get a pair or twa o' new socks for yer feet, or ye'll sune be like a body I kent in Houston parish——" Besides this, to a lonely man whose temper sometimes gave way by contact with an unfeeling world outside, it was always a comfort to have some one to scold. Mistress Izet knew his constitution and did not speak back, but gave him physic; moreover, she was always telling him things, and even when he did not care to listen to her talk she was there. These matters had passed through his mind in vague procession while he was putting on his clothes, and now he began to see them in a clearer light. Mere monetary considerations are not everything in the lot of a human being. He had not been aware that Janet's presence was to any great extent a comfort to him till he commenced deliberately to think about the probability of losing it. Isaac had reached this point in his ruminations, when the parrot screamed, "There's Janet," and with that personage on his mind he naturally turned his head to be greeted with an eldrich laugh, as if the uncanny creature knew his thoughts. What if Mr. Congalton went away altogether, as he said was likely? The household would be broken up, and the place taken probably by the Bleachfield people, who would do their own gardening. Janet might go to that "randy" woman, her sister, and Zedie would not weave a stroke as long as her money lasted. As for him, he could get a cog at the table of Sandy Munn or William Caughie. Sandy was a dyker, and had an immoderately large and needy family in which there could be no repose. Then again the thought of William Caughie's Sabbatic face and attenuated red nose bestridden by the horn specs confronting him at every meal aggravated him into articulate utterance.

"No, by the man!" he said, "no." This was his one form of abjuration when speaking under excitement. If things could go on as they were, he felt he could be more thankful for his mercies than ever he had been before. Who would put up with the parrot as Janet had done, or indeed, for that matter, who would put up with himself?

"Isaac, Isaac, let the bruit awa'." The gardener put past his pipe. Then he rose and went over to the cage.

"No," he said, speaking to the bird with an unusually grave expression of face, "we maunna be separated, you and me. We canna mak' new friends at oor time o' day."

The bird evidently concluded that his master was in a conversational mood, and that it would not be consistent with sociable fitness that the talk should be all on one side, so it set its voice to the soft high tones of the governess' voice, and commenced to sing — "Up in the morning's no for me, up in the morning ear — ley." Then coming down to the normal pitch, it screamed with a flash of excitement in its black eyes — "Isaac, there's Janet. Irr ye there?"

As a matter of coincidence this was true, for at that moment the housekeeper appeared at the garden gate.

"Your parritch is dished and on the table," she said; "dinna stan' there palarvering wi' that bruit till they're dead cauld."

Isaac was glad to be brought back from the thought of uncongenial possibilities by the voice of his old friend, and was nothing loath to obey the rude summons. The cogitations of the morning had brought into the life of this lonely man new thoughts and new feelings, which seemed to trend entirely to one result. He took the cage in his hand. "Oo — ay," he said, "we maun tak' time to think farder o't, my pretty Poll. We have been pushed into a bonny maze this morning, but ony maze that ever I have seen had aye ae ootlet."

This remark provoked the parrot into a rasping paroxysm of laughter, which continued till they were half-way up the outside stair.

CHAPTER XI

A JOURNALIST ON FURLOUGH

GEORGE CONGALTON had returned from London on a working furlough. He had a retaining fee, and a white card, to write on any subject he thought would be interesting; but he was to hold himself in readiness, in the event of being required for foreign service. His book — *Sketches of a Special Correspondent in the Recent War* — was daily attracting fresh notice, and drawing forth golden opinions from the reviews; but though his name was in all the journals, his fame had not yet reached Kilspindie. Mr. Lonen, the school-master, had read the book and passed it on to the minister; but to all others he was simply — Dr. Congalton's brother. Though a Scotchman by birth, he had spent most of his life in connection with the metropolitan press. It is true he began his journalistic career in Scotland, but at an early period he was removed from the Scottish weekly on which he was engaged to manage a news-agency in London. It was the early days of such agencies, and Congalton distinguished himself by doing most of the work with his own hand. They had numerous correspondents who sent in the dry bones on which he put the literary flesh. His pen was facile; his imagination impressive. Humour he had, but it was serviceable only for private use. He knew too well the limits of a news-agency to try it there. Congalton had a wonderful instinct for the space value of news. He understood the lines on which public interest could be roused, and the amount of sentiment that might safely be used to satisfy it. Let it be a fire, a colliery accident, a railway disaster, or an item from the seat of war — anything picturesque or appalling, six lines of a telegram in his hands was good for half a column that would stir the emotions and hasten the blood. On the other hand, a column of well-written matter would fall into a paragraph, without regret, or the sacrifice of an essential fact, if the public wanted it not. His readiness of resource procured him a tempting offer for service in troublous times abroad. There were marvellous stories told of him as a war correspondent — under what difficulties he wrote — his long and exhaustive rides to post and telegraph office. These things were chronicled afterwards, but no one dreamed of them on reading the brief but comprehensive telegrams, and the brilliant descriptive articles that followed; there was grasp, generalship, a sense of military dash and movement in his writing which drew the eyes of Europe to the war columns of the *Morning Despatch*. Yet this clever pressman was the most unmethodical of men. He made notes at all times and everywhere — on the backs of old envelopes, on blank pages of letters, margins of newspapers, or indeed on any scrap of paper that lay to his hand in camp or battle-field, but how these were reckoned with afterwards and brought to useful account remained his own secret. While enjoying change of scene at Kilspindie, and freed from the exigencies of daily responsibility, he did not remain idle. He amused himself with

rod and gun, but true to his training, his eye
and ear were ever on the alert for " copy."
Indeed he was himself astonished at the wealth
of material that lay around him. When once
his curiosity was aroused he was not slow to
question and investigate, and this came to be
talked of at the Brig-end.

The candle-maker declared he would " speir
the bottom oot o' a kitty byne," but the cartwright had a ready and enlightened defence,
which received the adherent applause of Jaik
Short and Tilly Brogan the merchant. " Na,"
the cartwright had said, " I am nane again
looking into things — the man that has the
courage to speir questions is aye learnin'.
Some folk'll no ask questions for fear o' showing their ain ignorance; we're a' i' the schule
yet. Even I'm no abune carrying a satchel
mysel'."

Congalton's northern contributions to the
Despatch were remarkably clever, and attracted
the attention of literary London. Some of
them found their way into the county paper,
and were read in Kilspindie. The studies were
from life, and touched familiar ground, but no

one recognized himself, and so far as the
writer could discover nobody suspected their
authorship.

One day while in search of something in his
daughter's school-room he came across the
local paper containing copious extracts from
one of his own sketches. It was marked on
each side of the headline by a cross, and the
name, written on the paper itself, was " Miss
Hetty Hazlet." Of the governess herself Congalton had seen but little. His daughter paid
him daily visits, and he was pleased with the
progress she was making. Her manners were
gentle and lady-like, and he felt sure this was the
result of contact with a refined and cultured
mind. Having discovered this marked newspaper he proceeded to speculate on the coincidence. To Congalton this fresh departure in
journalism was a species of recreation which lay
in the line of his own liking. The new power
was a discovery which surprised and pleased
him. Following this revelation there came a
desire for sympathy — for a confidant who could
stand on the other side of the hedge, as it were,
and cry things over to him. The feeling be-

trayed a strange vanity amounting to feebleness, and was a curious trait in the character of a reserved and self-trustful man. At one time he had thought of confiding his secret to the school-master. Mr. Lonen was in some ways a colourless man. He held the opinion that there was little prose writing since the Elizabethan period worthy of the name of literature. He himself wrote sonnets. He laughed and wept in sonnets. There was no occasion too blithe or sacred for them, though they were mostly in the minor key. He called them "fourteen line epics," and covered the landscape with them; even Dr. Congalton's memory did not escape. Yet it was not wholly on this account that this mighty trust was withheld from him; however wrong his views and however wretched his verse might be, he could keep a secret from his neighbours —his wife could not. The crossed newspaper had arrested Congalton. What about this Miss Hazlet? She was an educated person, and had read portions of at least one of these articles.

He had reached this point when Mistress Izet knocked at the study door and announced the

Rev. Mr. Maconkey. The minister had made a ceremonious call once before after his brother's death, but they had not met since Congalton's return. Maconkey was a tall, cadaverous man with a limited mental horizon, fairly suited as a frame for his orthodoxy. Natural bias of conscience almost brought him out at the Disruption, but his mother put him on a preparatory course of spare diet which wrecked his determination. Later in life he was at times inclined to be dolorous in his preaching, but as the manse maid (she was a woman of fifty) told Mrs. Lonen, the "mistress always gied him a Collisen's pill on the Fridays to lichten his liver."

Maconkey's habits of study were peculiar. For one whole day in every seven he darkened his study window and lay on his stomach on a couch arranging his sermon for the following Sunday. He was what was called a doctrinal preacher, and one of his favourite doctrines was infant baptism. Congalton could not help recalling an incident narrated by the schoolmaster bearing on this subject while listening good-naturedly to the solemn, formal, introductory words of his visitor. The previous ploughman at Mossfennan, having an imperative reason for visiting the manse, was inadvertently shown into the study on one of the minister's "dark days." It was an "eerie reception," he said, "in the licht o' day," but he was trying to compose himself "i' the mirk," when suddenly a tall masterful figure gathered itself from the couch into stern and interrogative erectness The frightened ploughman was retiring in undignified haste, fearing that the prince of darkness, from whom he had been taught to flee, was at his heels. The pursuing voice, however, was the minister's.

"Weel, Saunders?"

"Dod, sir, ye gaed me a deev — an — an — unco fricht, I assure ye."

The minister opened a wing of the shutters and let the light in temperately on the ploughman's scared face.

"It was very inconsiderate of the maid. But state your business briefly, Saunders, for, to speak truly, I am busy to-day."

"Have ye no heard the steer?" Saunders inquired.

"Steer about what?"

"Aboot the guidwife. Ye kent, of course, that she was wechty i' the fit, but she brocht hame a bonny bit wean a week by on Tuesday."

"Then ye'll be thinking about the solemn rite of baptism," said the minister.

"That's aboot it," replied Saunders. "The wife's no strong, and I thocht a waff o' fresh air frae the sea wi' her mither at Troon wud gie her heartin, but she'll no budge a fit till the bit thing's kirstened."

"Weel, Saunders, I hope your views are quite clear on this all-important question of infant baptism. Do you not think your wife was right?"

"I canna say she wis, sir, but then ye see weemen hinna minds like you and me — it's clean superstectious a'thegither, but it doesna do to thraw wi' them when they're in her state. I thocht ye wud maybe come owre by i' the gloamin, and scale a drap or twa o' watter on the bit face."

As Congalton sat listening with an air of respectful attention to the deep tones of the minister's voice, he thought of the indignant interruption which ensued, and of the severe course of disciplinary handling which ultimately brought the humble ploughman with trembling to the pulpit steps to enrol his child in the register of the Church Militant. To speak with candour, the Rev. Mr. Maconkey did not relish the duty which had brought him to Broomfields, but a sense of justice impelled him to perform it. The story of Miss Hazlet's secret meeting with her cousin had lost none of its disreputable characteristics by passing through the augmentive mind of Mrs. Lonen. She told her husband, but was so vexed by his indifference that Nancy Beedam and Mrs. Caughie, as her next neighbours, got it under monitorial restrictions, " Dinna say a word, but watch for yoursel's."

After this she let two days pass, but seeing no outcome, she confided it to the minister's wife. The manse was a kind of central telephonic exchange (though such an institution was then unknown), to which all tales involving the parish morals travelled, and Mrs. Maconkey was the person to whom the gossips contrived to get switched on. In point of fact, Mrs. Lonen was not the first to convey the story to the manse. Mrs. Maconkey had already questioned the governess and discovered the truth. Poor Hetty was dreadfully shocked at the construction put upon her simple cousinly act.

What if Mr. Congalton had already heard the story? If he believed it he could not consider her a fit teacher or companion for his daughter. How could she live in the place? She must tell him, and resign her situation. These were her first thoughts while her face burned with shame and indignation, but her prudent, matronly adviser deprecated hasty action, so that the duty of defending the innocent and rectifying this wrong fell upon the minister. Mr. Maconkey narrated the incident with needless gravity. This village life seemed of huge importance to his mind. Such defection, if true, would to him have had almost tragical significance.

Congalton acknowledged the minister's good offices with becoming courtesy. He saw his visitor to the gate, and returned to put the closing sentences to the article on which he was engaged. There was humour even in the so-called tragedies of these rural communities. He thought of the friendless girl, however, and admitted that the humour would be more apparent when the tragedies were impersonal. He heard Eva's silvery laugh in the hall, and knew the governess and she had returned from their afternoon stroll. In truth, Hetty had passed the time with Mrs. Maconkey in the manse garden till the minister's return. Congalton rang the bell, and asked to see Miss Hazlet.

Hetty came in pale, but self-possessed. She had the bravery of an honest conscience.

"I am sorry you have been vexed about the gossip of these silly neighbours of ours," he began lightly. "Mr. Maconkey has told me all, and I think it was very proper of you to see your cousin; the misfortune for both was that you had to see him under circumstances that permitted of misunderstanding."

"I did not dream of misunderstanding," Hetty said. "The poor boy sought my help, and I was anxious to do the best I could for him."

"Naturally. Mr. Maconkey tells me of your cousin's return to his father; he seems to have profited by your advice. It was worth running some risk to bring about that. But do not think ill news travels fastest. I might not have known of this apprehension but for your minister, whereas I heard from several lips immediately on my return of your courage in saving my daughter at your own peril. The poor parochial mind has few resources — it is natural that the affairs of others should bulk largely in it for good or evil. You must bear with and forgive it. Now let us speak of something else. I was in the school-room by accident to-day and saw a local paper addressed to you with an article marked."

"Yes," she replied, looking at him with clear eyes, "my sister sent it, and several others; I have read them all."

"May I ask if they interested you?"

"They did." Congalton was carried forward by a smile that had more behind it.

"Now, I am unreasonably inquisitive," he said, laughing; "but had you any suspicions as to the authorship of these articles?"

"Well," she said frankly, "I knew your connection with the *Despatch*, and inferred from internal evidence that they were yours."

"You know Scottish life and character well?"

"I am a daughter of the manse," she said simply.

"Ah, that means much. Well, I have a curious interest in this queer place and its people, but when writing I come to a dead wall at times over difficulties of dialect, and other matters about which I may take the liberty to consult you. Having found me out, I shall trust you to keep the secret."

The interview closed with a formal assurance that he was well satisfied with her work as Eva's instructor. Hetty went to her bedroom and found relief in tears, but they were the tears of April, with the sun and a brief space of blue behind; for the crisis of resigning her situation and leaving a child she really loved had been averted.

CHAPTER XII

KILSPINDIE

To a writer with an observant eye and a cosmopolitan mind Kilspindie parish and village really had many features that were worthy of notice. The front of the candle-maker's workshop at the Brig-end was the place where, in genial weather, the mature village mind was nurtured by the mutual exchange of such ideas and inspirations as might move it under the passing influences of the hour. From this point the eye had an unembarrassed survey of the river, to the stepping stones leading from the Holm to the Manse brae. Between these points and below Lippy Barbour's bleachfield there was a deep pool, which used to be a favourite resting place for the salmon, but Lippy's acid had spoiled all that. Any one coming across old Bowlie Dempster, in the

lapse of rheumatics, at Brig-end would be sure
of one fishing story at least. Bowlie would lay
his chin on the parapet, with one eye fixed on
the salmon pool, and the other on the pro-
jecting bleachfield wall — for he could see two
ways at a time — and tell about the "burning
of the waters" in the days when leistering was
thought no sin. In a fair round of poaching
experience this pool was the central glory,
for it nearly cost him his life. But it was a
story he loved to set Angus Pringle, the smith,
to tell.

"I was just kenlin' the smiddy fire in the grey
o' the mornin'," — Congalton had brought the
two worthies together, and Bowlie was smirking
and fidging to hear his friend tell the exploit
once again, — "when my frien' Bowlie here comes
in a' oot o' breath, wi' een as big as saucers."

"Hear till him," interrupted Dempster,
"canny before the gentleman." — "'Dod,' says
I, 'ye have surely risen aff yer wrang side
this morning;' but the long and the short
o't was the man had seen a salmon i' the Park-
yett pool."

"Tell the size o't," cried Dempster with

anticipating eagerness; but the smith waved the interruption aside as premature.

"So efter gien his leister twa turns on the grunstane, Bowlie took to his heels and I followed at my leisure. I stood back and waited on the brig, but could see fine frae the twist o' the man's body that the beast was still there."

"Just whaur I left it," said Dempster, "wi' its side again' a bit stane, thinking it was holed; but the funny bit 's coming; go on, smith. and tell what happened syne."

"Weel, while I was looking I sees him taking aim — and — bang gangs the leister."

"Clean through the fish," was Bowlie's eager interpolation.

"Oh, through the fish fair eneugh," the smith admitted without a qualm. "Things were slack efter-hin for aboot the space o' four ticks o' the nock, when a steer begude that ended in a deevil o' a turry-wurry between man and beast; but I saw fine frae the first hoo it wud be — there was a rive, and in plunges Bowlie head first still haudin' on by the leister." Here Dempster slapped Congalton on the shoulder and laughed till the tears dropped on the smithy floor. Then he turned to the smith with the eagerness of a first hearing, and implored him to go on.

"Thinkin' the craitur wud droon," the smith resumed, "I dreeped frae the brig and eased the gallacies frae my shouthers as I ran, for I kent Bowlie couldna soom a stroke. There they were — fish, leister, and man — ragin' round and round the pool. Nanny Welsh, who had come oot to the garden wi' some hen's meat, says I cried till 'm to let go, but whether I did or whether I didna, he held on. Thinks I, my man, ye have carried war into the enemy's country. Gin yer so thrawn that ye winna let go, I'm no gaun to wat my skin for ye. Wi' that the beast gets kina tired."

"And still I hauds on," cried Dempster proudly.

"Yes, still ye hauds on, and I sees a bit smile on yer face as if ye were saying, ' Noo I've got the upper hand o' ye, wha's got the rynes noo?'"

"That's the smith's fancy," interrupted Dempster, rubbing his hands; "at times ye wud think he could mak' a po'm."

"Weel, at lang and last, the beast cam near the surface and turned his glittering belly to the rising sun, — the current brocht them into shawl watter, — and Bowlie, feeling the gravel under his knees, sprachled oot and brought his prize safe to the bank."

"What wecht?" demanded the poacher.

"Twenty-fower pound," responded the smith, "a' barrin' twa unces; it was weighed that morning on the merchant's scales."

Congalton could not discover that Kilspindie figured conspicuously as the scene of any great historical event. An incident occurred in the "Forty-five," but the Wheat Sheaf inn had the monopoly of it. This hostelry stood well back from the road, and had an open space in front for the convenience of vehicles on Sundays and market days. The building was single storey and thatched, with a window on one side of the entrance and two on the other. It was said Prince Charlie and a limited retinue had partaken of refreshment in the room with the two windows, and that he had kissed the great-aunt of Mrs. MacFarlane, the present occupant, in settlement of the "lawin." John Kidstoun, the village wright of the time, being a fair judge of morals, made a large kist when he heard the Pretender was in the vicinity into which he and his neighbours put their valuables. This they buried in the manse garden till he and his needy followers had passed into the next parish.

These facts were not written in any history, but they were on the mental tablets of the school-master, who had them from the lips of Kidstoun's son. In the cold, dark evenings of winter, when there was anything to talk about (as a rule little served), the men foregathered in the room with the single window. It was in this room Francie Dyack fainted and never came to; the belief was that this untoward event happened because they gave him a drink of water after his race without thinking to put either meal or whisky in it. Francie had been visiting his sweetheart in the Haugh at the back of the Braes on halloween, and for a near cut was returning through the plantain where Granny Dalap hanged herself. On nearing the ominous spot a human skull seemed to kindle into awesome vividness among the bare branches of the tree from which the suicide's body had been cut down. The eyes were glazed and motionless, the nose a corrupt hole, and the mouth, from which the tongue protruded, had a ghastly grin. Francie was heard singing the 121st Psalm as he raged down the school brae, but on reaching the inn he had only breath left to mumble out what is now known of the event before he fainted. Only William Madden and Andrew Frame knew the secret, and they had it on their conscience as a crime to their dying day. They had hollowed a turnip, made a frightsome face on it, put a lighted candle inside, and hung it on Granny Dalap's tree to amuse or hasten the step — as might happen — of any one who chanced to pass that way. Andrew Frame went to the antipodes afterwards, but his companion settled down soberly at home — to drink. It was William Madden, who when the minister checked him for being under the influence of whisky at eleven o'clock in the forenoon, said, "Man, if ye tak' it early ye'll fin' the guid o't a' day."

The rendezvous of the young people of Kilspindie was Elsie Craig's well at Millend.

This well was shaded in summer by an ancient
chestnut-tree, whose flower-spikes were un-
equalled for size and beauty for ten miles round,
taking the candle-maker's workshop as the
centre of the circumference. This precise way
of stating the case was due to Matha Fairley,
the Yorkhill forester, and as no better informed
man ever contradicted him his way of putting
it became the settled belief. The water in Elsie
Craig's well had many good qualities, but it
was said to take the fullest cleansing virtue out
of soap in its application to baby linen and
weaver's aprons. On summer evenings village
maidens went forth to draw it. The well, being
deep, cans and stoups had to be let down by
a rope and cleek, and as strength and nerve
were required for this, it was not unnatural
that chivalrous swains should be by to help
the maidens in their task. The half of the
male villagers who had entered the fold of
matrimony had commenced their wooing here;
and, as might be expected in such a precarious
world, not a few love-lights, that had been
kindled under the chestnut-tree had been
quenched in shame. When the men-folk mar-

ried they said good-bye to the well, and met afterwards at the Brig-end or at Mrs. Mac-Farlane's change-house. Some of the older men, whose years gave them confidence of speech, used to delight in telling their courting exploits at the well. Robin Brough had fought the merchant's salesman for the hand of Teeny Middlemas. The vanquished salesman, not feeling equal to the continuance of a militant courtship, sought employment in the Old Victualling Store at Galston, leaving the prize to the victor. After this Robin's candle frames were kept busy, for Teeny was what was called a "dressy buddy," and on first days even eclipsed the minister's lady herself. Indeed the confidence of being better dressed than anybody else on the Sabbath day was said to give her a feeling of inward tranquillity that religion itself was powerless to bestow. Chronic rheumatics, however, had been the instrument in the hand of an admonishing Providence of tempering her vanity, and affording her husband the meditative and conversational leisure he now enjoyed.

Jean Templeton, a shy maiden, thinking the

lads had gone, went out one evening to draw water. Her stoup was slipping from her hand, and she herself might have gone down after it, had not William Caughie, who had hidden behind the chestnut, hopeful of seeing Jean, caught her in his arms, and restored her equanimity. He kissed her without trouble, so he said, though her explanation that she was useless with fright was reasonable. It was known that before this Jean preferred the foreman bleacher, but the marriage took place on the fifth Friday thereafter. In early days William used to tell this story with some pride; advancing years, however, had taken the glamour out of it. He ceased entirely to refer to the matter when he took to the wearing of horn specs after the introduction of the Reform Bill. Though generation after generation of the villagers had paused for a time at this oasis, and amused or refreshed themselves before graduating into the dual state, the old well was still surrounded in the summer gloaming, as before, by the young of both sexes, feeling after the fuller life — the well-spring of love being as inexhaustible as its own crystal waters.

When Congalton found his articles on Scottish rural life and character had awakened public interest, his old instinct of knowing how to give what was wanted revived under the sense that the field from which he could draw was wide and full. His pictures were cameos — embracing the colour, form, and atmosphere of Scottish scenery. Deftly thrown forward on this picturesque, natural background were the characters, actions, and thoughts of men and women, giving human interest to the whole. Though his men inclined to politics, and an occasional dram, and his women to gossip and, at times, scandal, they were on the whole a religious people. Any one going through the village street at nine o'clock on a Sunday morning could not get beyond the voice of psalms in the exercise of worship.

Old Jeames Goudie, who lived by himself in a single apartment at Millend, represented an earlier time, for he had this salutary exercise every morning. Jeames was very deaf, and before singing always "read the line." He had brought up a large family of sons, who vexed him with their extravagant, idle habits.

He used to complain that they were "brisk
at gaun oot at nicht, but aye lost their gate
comin' hame." Nancy Beedam once heard him
say — "It wud have been mair profitable gin I
had buried the lot o' ye when ye were young
— aye spend-spending and never dune." This
remark had been made under provocation, but
Nancy never forgot it, they had all gone to
the kirkyard before him.

While making free with contemporary life and
character Congalton was not unmindful to draw
on senile memories for customs and beliefs that
had now become effete. Oddities in the
marriage, baptismal, and burial services were to
his liking. Belief in the supernatural, even in
the younger generation, was not yet entirely
stamped out. Death warnings — the ticking of
a watch or a knock at the bed-head in the
sick-room — were held as unerring portents
of approaching death. The wild horse with
the clanking shoon had been heard on the
hillside at midnight above Mossfennan by
several of the older inhabitants before the
plague of cholera visited the village. Davit
Saunders, the Blacklaw shepherd, returning

from the uplands one night late saw Tammas Scougall with a bundle of mole-traps over his shoulder. Tammas passed silently, and made no response to his neighbour's "guid e'en," but remembering afterwards that Tammas had been in bed ill for several days, Saunders took to his heels and ran home in fright. Next morning he heard that the mole-catcher had passed away at the very hour he encountered him on the hillside. Lexie Findlater had seen a whole "cleckan" of fairies one moonlight night "loupin' the ragweeds" in a field in front of the farm where she was at service. Her cousin, Nan Pinkerton, now known as the "spae-wife o' the Haugh," also in service at an adjoining farm, was for a time shadowed by a "brownie" who did the rougher housework for her while she was sleeping. One night— meaning kindly — Nan left a dish of sowens and milk by the fireside for the considerate worker, but he never returned.

With these and similar materials of fact and folklore available, Congalton had little need to go beyond the parish. According to habit, his study table was littered with old envelopes embracing scraps of scenery done on the spot, sketches of character, superstitious customs and beliefs, together with odd sayings and idioms of local growth. The governess, now in full sympathy with his work, and in possession of his secret, thinking his manner of proceeding might be improved, suggested the classification of his notes by the aid of an index. This method she initiated for him, but it was not a success. In theory he admitted it was correct and business-like, but it led to constraint and formality. These scraps had their own individuality of suggestion, recalling the thought or inspiration of the moment. While the governess's business-like system commended itself to his judgment, it led him by a process of self-analysis to the conclusion that changes either in his habits of life or in his methods of work could not now safely be made.

CHAPTER XIII

MRS. COWIE'S LIBRARY

WHEN Mrs. Lonen told the minister's wife the story confided to her by Mrs. Cowie, neither of these good ladies suspected that the farmer's wife had anything but the purest motives behind it. The minister also entertained the same belief. He knew that Dr. Congalton by the terms of his will intended, and desired, that his brother should form a matrimonial connection with the Cowie family. It seemed therefore reasonable on their part, if they reciprocated the doctor's wish, that they should have a care about the proper upbringing of Mr. Congalton's child. Mr. Maconkey considered it his duty to relieve Mrs. Cowie's anxiety on this important question by telling her the truth at once. Further, he informed her that he had explained the matter

fully to the child's father, lest the story in its
original colouring should reach him and prove
detrimental to Miss Hazlet's good name. He
ventured to express his conviction that she
(Mrs. Cowie) would be pleased to know that
her surmises, while perfectly justifiable from
ocular evidence, were, in point of fact, ground-
less. She felt it was clear, from the minister's
trustful and straightforward explanation, that
he did not suspect her of having any ulterior
motive. Indeed, he had excused her solicitude
by delicately revealing his knowledge of the
late doctor's desire for a closer relationship
between the two families. Mrs. Cowie received
these assurances with mixed feelings. She was
comforted by being misunderstood, and by the
minister's confiding sympathy. It is true she
believed from what she herself saw that there
was a moral screw loose somewhere in the
governess's character, but for her own purposes
the wish was father to the belief; and, as her
plans were somewhat frustrated by the disproof
of this conviction, there was little satisfaction
in it. After that aggravating Sunday, when
her husband had thoughtlessly invited young

Mitchell to dinner she had indulged in some plain speaking. Windy-yett, whom she characterized, perhaps fairly, as "a ram-stam man," had been solidly set in his place. He had feebly retaliated by saying he would give the halter to her, as the doctor had left a "kittle powny to lead." She dare not, however, take such high ground with Bell. She explained with judicious delicacy to that young lady the full meaning of the doctor's will. Bell was tickled into questioning laughter over the oddness of the situation.

"How can the doctor will his brother to me?" she inquired, wondering how far law could go. Mrs. Cowie conceded that such a thing might not be quite according to law, but that where a man had left siller with stipulations, there was a moral obligation on the parties who accepted of it to respect his wishes. Knowing the exalted and improvident sentiments of youth, she did not reveal to Bell the questionable schemes that were taking shape in her own mind. She laid stress rather on her daughter's natural attractions. Her arguments were specious and alluring. Bell was young, and could lose nothing by waiting a year or two. The happiest time of a young woman's life was when men were competing to win her. She had simply to wait and choose. If she were to be asked to take the place of governess or companion to Mr. Congalton's daughter, and charmed him with her fine manners into making a proposal of marriage, it would be like a play. Bell laughed responsively. " Think too of bringing the doctor's siller into the family, just as he willed it — I declare it's like what ye read o' in story books."

Bell was really amused, and her mother left the romance to germinate. Day by day the idea of becoming a heroine, with suitors at her feet pleading for her hand, took deeper hold of the young woman's fancy. She saw, from un-mistakable attentions, that Willie Mitchell could be had any day, but her mother's words had stirred her imagination, and it in turn begat new desires. She was young, as her mother had said, and wanted a fuller experience. The more she thought of it the more the hunger for conquests took possession of her. Under this access of sentiment she concluded that to marry the first man who offered would be to impoverish her youth, and rob life of its due meed of romance. A maidenhood of prose, with but a single stanza of poetry in it, was out of the question. It would be such fun to see this middle-aged suitor on his knees begging her to become his wife. Though their fortunes, as her mother had explained, were somewhat mixed up, she would not be bound to marry if she did not love him. Besides, would not Willie Mitchell think all the more of her if she had rejected another man for his sake?

To find that fortune would not open the door for Bell as governess in Mr. Congalton's household, when she had brought her daughter to this reasonable and compliant frame of mind, was deeply disappointing to the designing mother. Bell was flighty, and might suffer change of mood. Still Mrs. Cowie was not the woman to be paralyzed in purpose by one failure. She had a large and hopeful mind. The governess was apparently safe in the meantime, but the light of Windy-yett was not to be obscured under a bushel. She had not directed her husband to buy a new horse for nothing. The lighter animal, now set free from field work, was not intended to wax fat in the stall for want of exercise. It had been a favourable summer, and there was promise of an ample harvest, moreover the interest of Bell's " tocher" was a substantial reality. The merchant experienced the opportuneness of this fact at a time of year when the tide of credit was at its lowest ebb. At least twice a week they drove to his door to make purchases, and while they showed the horse's paces, and Bell's skill in handling whip and reins on their way to the village, they invariably took the brac opposite Broomfields leisurely on their return. Mr. Congalton once, catching the maternal eye, bowed to them from his study window as they passed.

"Smile, Bell," whispered Mrs. Cowie, nudging her daughter under the rug. "Don't ye see the gentleman bowing to ye ?" The defect about Bell Cowie's face, in her mother's eyes, was that it did not wear a perennial smile. It was a fresh, plump, oval face, with hazel-grey eyes. In repose the chin was a trifle heavy, but the heaviness was lightened when she showed her sound white teeth and smiled.

Bell bowed back gracefully and obeyed the motherly injunction.

"Aye keep smiling." Mrs. Cowie had been encouraging the use of this weapon of late. "No man can resist ye if ye show him thae bonny white teeth, and that blyth humoursome curl aboot the een. That noo —" for Bell was giving fair illustration of the expression of countenance her mother wished her to wear.

During the inactive period, when the farmer looks to the sun and moon and the genial airs of heaven to bring to golden fruition the work that he has initiated by ploughing and sowing, Mrs. Cowie and her daughter had a gay time driving hither and thither, paying visits and making purchases. Broomfields somehow always lay on their route in going or returning. Mrs. Cowie's purposes were persevering and hopeful. There was no other person on the parochial horizon so likely to interest this "widow man" as Bell.

One day at Alec Brodie's corner they met the object of their solicitude returning with his gun. He lifted his hat politely and made to pass, but Bell was ordered to draw rein while the mother took speech in hand. They were going (it was

166

the decision of the moment) on the following day to the rose-show at Kilkenzie, and she would be pleased if he would allow his daughter to accompany them. As her husband was also going, she was sorry there was not room in the gig for the governess, but Bell was "mortal fond o' little anes, and would take real guid care o' her." Bell blushed and smiled lightly at her mother's audacity, and looked none the worse for it. She was not in love with the man, and could afford to practise the art by which her mother made her believe she could fascinate men. Was it possible this poor middle-aged gentleman should yet be brought to her feet? Bell wondered if the slight pause which ensued was the result of embarrassed admiration. On the other part Congalton was amused by the efforts of this crystalline diplomat to encompass a literal fulfilment of his brother's wishes.

"It is very good of you," he said, "but I am afraid I must ask you to excuse her to-morrow. Some other time when there is room for both I am sure it will be a pleasure for them to drive out with you."

Mrs. Cowie, with her own private purposes in

mind, did not quite relish the concluding part of his reply, but she spoke encouragingly to her daughter.

" Bell," she said, as they turned into the parish road, " I'm thinking the doctor had some skill o' his ain flesh and bluid when he made that will; did ye no see, when Mr. Congalton pairted wi' us, how his een settled on your face as he lifted his hat? "

Two days later Congalton received a letter perfumed to obtrusiveness. It was written in Mrs. Cowie's name, but the composition and the hand were Bell's. She reverted to their previous meeting, and expressed regret that she had omitted to ask him to come over and see the library she had recently purchased for her daughter at the displenishing sale of a man who was book-learned and a great scholar. If Thursday afternoon would suit she would take it as a great kindness to have his valuable opinion of her purchase. These unconventional manœuvres were interesting. The little rural comedy was developing. Why should he not go? He good-naturedly returned a verbal message by the bearer of the letter that he would go along

on the day named and look at the books with
pleasure. This, then, was his vulnerable point.
Mrs. Cowie had secretly cherished this belief
when she went to the roup — her purchase had
not been money thrown away, as her husband
thought. If the books brought him to Windy-
yett it would not be her own fault, or Bell's, if
he did not often return. The books certainly
brought him, and having a gentlemanly sense of
humour, they gratified it; but the inspection was
also instructive, in the sense that it revealed the
contents of an educated Scottish farmer's book-
case of the period. There were twelve volumes of
the *Agricultural Magazine*, Baxter's *Saint's Rest*,
Sermons by the Rev. Andrew Fairservice, *The
Confession of Faith*, *Tainsh on the Four Gospels*,
The Crook in the Lot, the first series of Tait's
Edinburgh Magazine, several text-books in
medicine, and, beside the Smiddy-yard treasures,
all Bell's school prizes were arrayed with purposeful intent. Mrs. Cowie watched her visitor's face
with absorbing eyes. There could be no literary
attraction equal to this in the parish.

"Well," she inquired eagerly, after he had
taken down volume after volume of such

tomes as appealed to his fancy, and examined them.

"A solid, and, to me at least, an uncommon collection of books." In truth he could say no less.

Mrs. Cowie was charmed. Could there be any fuller or fairer evidence of her own sagacity? but her interest became more acute as he took out Bell's prizes, one after the other, and scanned the inside for the subjects that had exercised her mind in competing for them. She was trying to follow his thoughts through the advancing stages of wonderment as to how a farmer's daughter had reached this perfection of education; then, as if to explain, she became articulate. "I declare it taks a lash o' siller to make a leddy noo-a-days." Bell blushed honestly, and begged her mother not to trouble Mr. Congalton with such needless details. He was served with tea in " quality " fashion before he left.

"Your brother, the doctor, was no tea-hand," Mrs. Cowie explained, "he was fond o' a gless o' toddy wi' the guidman when he stepped owre after the day's visiting was dune. He used to

tak' Bell on his knee when she was a wee thing,
and got her to put a single piece o' loaf sugar in
his first tumbler before she gaed to bed. He
was that humoursome, he would say that the
wee bit fingers gave the toddy a fine flavour.
Na, are you sure you would prefer tea, the
sperits are quite handy?" Mrs. Cowie always
thought a travelled man would like spirits and
water on a hot day. Congalton told them
affably how he had spent days in the saddle
under a broiling sun, his only refreshment being
cold tea without cream or sugar.

"Surce the day!"

Mrs. Cowie concluded it would be a "gey
wersh drink." Bell handed round the cakes,
and told him with a captivating glance how she
had heard he had written a book about the
wars. A book by one who had actually seen
a battle must be really delightful. "Oh my!"
she would like to read such a book! Before he
was aware Congalton had promised to send
her a copy. Bell was radiant with thanks and
smiles. Had the love philtre already begun to
work? What a fine gracious and chivalrous
manner he had, and how different from the self-

conscious awkwardness of rustic swains! She was afraid when he came to propose she might find herself in love with him after all. Bell sighed softly behind her newly-ringed hand, thinking of poor Willie Mitchell.

Before leaving Mrs. Cowie informed her visitor that he wouldn't find many books in Kilspindie. "The country folks are but poor readers," she said, "they never buy books. I may say this library of Bell's is the only one in the neighbourhood; and if there is onything in it that would be of use to you ye're welcome to the use o't."

Returning home by the green lanes in the quiet of that early autumn gloaming, Congalton came to see that the matter was going just a trifle beyond the verge of legitimate comedy, and resolved to visit Mr. Sibbald next day at his place of business in the county town. Two days later, while Richard Cowie and the "orra man" were at the moss loading peats, they heard the postman's whistle, and on looking up Cowie saw that functionary at the march gate on the moorland road making gestures.

"It's a letter," he remarked, straightening his

back and shading his eyes with a grimy hand, "some mair o' that patent manure dirt. It'll be addressed to the mistress like enough, for she likes to study thae things. What for does the craitur no' tak' it on to the hoose?" The lad at the march gate, however, continued to whistle and gesticulate with something in his right hand, and the orra man was ordered to run over and see what it was. It was a letter addressed, not to Mrs. Cowie, but to her husband, and bore the imprint of Sibbald and Campbell, writers. Cowie directed the orra man to go on loading the peats while he turned his back to the sun and broke the seal. It was a long letter of four pages, written in Mr. Sibbald's own cramped hand. The farmer's thirst for the secret the letter contained was out of all proportion to his power of assuaging it. He had borne at least three-quarters of the labour involved in loading a cart of peats without turning a hair; now his back was clammy, and big drops of yellow perspiration swam from side to side of his ample chin as his head moved to various angles of acquisitiveness, yet he had not mastered the first page. It was something, he knew, about

Dr. Congalton's legacy — but what? He had already said to himself, " It would have been a sicht better they had never heard o' ony sic will." What good was it going to do them? " It had put Bell (meaning his wife) on her high horse, and was carrying her clean aff at the head wi' her leebrary o' books, her veesiting cairds, and what not — it was perfect vexatious." He went over to the logan stone, leant his back against the shady side, and held his letter so that angular rays of the westering sun fell softly athwart the jerky lines of the perplexing enigma. After an hour's hard reading he formed some hazy notion of its purport. On the whole it gave him a feeling of relief. The orra man, having waited for some time on his master, wondering what was the good of education (he was no scholar himself) if it took one man so long to find out another man's meaning when he put it in black and white. Cowie, having superintended the progress of the cart through the ruts and quags of the moss, left it safely on the solid moor road and took a near cut home.

Bell was reading Mr. Congalton's book aloud to her mother, who sat near her darning stockings with a contemplative smile. The farmer looked so heated and mysterious that his wife left her stockings, followed him " ben the house," and inquired if it was another " turn o' the water-brash."

" Na, na," he said, " it's news — news frae Mr. Sibbald," and he handed her the letter. Mrs. Cowie closed the door and snibbed it. Then they sat down side by side on the settle and endeavoured to extract the meaning from this camstrary document.

" I'll be danged," said Cowie, after suffering numerous contradictions, not too politely expressed, over his diagnosis of words. This imprecation betokened a condition of mind not habitual.

" Why not send for Bell; what is the use of her boarding schule edication if we canna get the use o't at a pinch?" Mrs. Cowie was not a woman to waste words when her husband talked nonsense. A momentary look over her specs, and a contraction of the corners of her light grey eyes, showed him he was interfering in a matter that required delicate handling.

Meantime Mrs. Cowie patiently plodded for-

ward and began to get under the wing of the
lawyer's meaning. The letter was couched in
formal and carefully studied terms. Its general drift was that Dr. Congalton's trustees had
recently met, and taken into consideration the
hampering clause in the will which practically
stood in the way of Miss Cowie marrying unless
she effected a union with Mr. Congalton, who
was not a marrying man. They thought this
was rather hard on a young lady of undoubted
natural attractions, more particularly as his
co-trustees were aware through him (Mr. Sibbald) that the testator's desire was to show his
regard for the family by making some provision
for the daughter. If Miss Cowie and her parents
desired it, with the consent of parties, they would
be prepared to modify the will, so as to allow
her the monetary benefit intended, without
binding the principal legatees to the unusual
condition at present attaching to it. The request, however, should come from the young
lady herself in writing if her parents approved.
Cowie, having abandoned all attempts at a
literal verbal rendering, took refuge in a general understanding of the letter, and sat waiting

patiently with a fairly contented expression of countenance. He was satisfied that Bell would have a clear third without any complication or contingency. He watched keenly for the dawn of an acquiescent look in his wife's eyes as she went back again and again to words and phrases whose meaning required confirmation. Indeed she could not but think there was some legal quirk at the bottom of this remarkable letter. Matters to her mind seemed prospering well enough as they were. Congalton had already found his way to the farm; he had presented Bell with his book; between her and the library there was every human probability of being yet able to realize her own and the late doctor's wishes; but, in the most pessimistic view, should he marry some one else, or get killed in the wars, there was always a chance of more money coming to Bell than if she signed her rights away.

"Dinna ye think, na, it's a gey fair offer?" inquired the husband, with soft eyes fixed hopefully on the inscrutable face.

"No," she exclaimed with decision, "I think it's nane a fair offer. There's a meaning in that

letter that neither you nor me understands."
She bounced from her seat. " See, here's paper
and ink for ye," she said; "just you sit doon and
answer it when ye're i' the tid, and tell the wily
lawyer that we'll e'en bide by the Doctor's
will."

CHAPTER XIV

LOVE-MAKING

SOME days after Richard Cowie had sent his reply to Mr. Sibbald, Willie Mitchell, desiring to test the reasonableness of his hopes before commencing the harvest, came home early from Kilburnie fair, where he had left Cowie and his wife. He repaired to Windy-yett, and found Bell picking fruit in the garden all alone. He had thought so intensely on his journey over, and had made so many finely-worded proposals to the encouraging air, that on arriving he was mentally exhausted and confused. This big, strong-limbed man was afraid, from Mrs. Cowie's manner on several occasions, but particularly during the recent visit when he had the felicity of dining with the family, that she was not quite favourable to his honest intentions. Bell, however, had at least not discouraged him, and it was his wish to see her alone and have a quiet hour with her without interruption before her parents returned. Bell's eyes sparkled, and her teeth shone as she saw the weather-bronzed "wooer" stalking down the gravelled path, between the high box-wood borders; but when she saw the unnatural gravity of the youthful face, and the pallor of suppressed feeling about the lines of the mouth, she felt inclined to run away. Willie Mitchell, as a bantering beau, frisking suggestively, but with unformed intentions, on the no-man's land between fun and sentiment, was delightful. But Willie Mitchell with a mind made up and a body charged to the lips with pent-up passion that might explode at any moment, while there was no one near to encourage by-play, made her wish she had accompanied her parents to the fair.

"You are home soon," she said, throwing the ribbons of her sun-bonnet behind her back that she might show the dainty earrings her mother had purchased in anticipation of the first money product of the legacy. Then she remembered that she did not look her best when her face was serious — and smiled.

" Ay, I'm home soon," he said, being in no mood to waste words.

" Were there many at the fair ?" she inquired, stooping over her work.

" Oh, a heap o' folk as usual — you're unco' busy the day."

" No that busy."

" Ye'll get sunstroke, Bell; come awa' into the summer-house here, and rest ye."

" I'll run up to the hoose first wi' the berries," she cried, laughing, and tripped off through the garden gate with the fruit. What Bell wanted was time to think. Was this her first conquest ? Was it not her mother's teaching that a young woman of her attractions should have many such before she made choice ? Nanny Suther-land made no secret of the fact that she had three — and she was plain. Why should she think of Nanny Sutherland just then ? Nannie had turned real religious before her marriage. At the " kirkin' " she had left a plum-pudding in the pot to simmer, and all the way to the kirk she had it on her mind for fear the water should boil in ; but, as she said, the minister's text was " richt heartnin " " Cast thy burden on the Lord."

" Weel, I just did that, and let the pudding tak'
its chance." Bell laughed at the thought of thus
relieving herself of Willie Mitchell, and her
white teeth gleamed in her own looking-glass.
At the moment she was up in her little bedroom
adjusting and pinning up her refractory back
hair. She was not quite convinced that Nanny's
text applied to her present circumstances. If
burden there were, she inclined to take it on her
own plump shoulders. Bell tried her smile in
varying degrees of broadness until, becoming
conscious of the absurdity of her conduct, she
laughed at her own reflection — that, she concluded, — mockingly, the fresh, red lips just
revealing her white teeth — will be enough for
Willie Mitchell. But what was there to laugh
at? Who could dare to laugh or smile either
at a man with a tragic face like yon? It was
enough to bring tears to one's eyes. Then she
laughed once more at the thought of tears for
a young and hale man such as she had left in
the summer-house. "Ay," she said, coming
within hail, " and ye didna like the fair."

" Oh, I liket the fair weel enough."

" And why did ye hurry awa' frae't ? "

"Because — because, Bell, to tell ye the honest truth, I liket something else far better. Bell, will ye come and sit doon?" She started back from his strong arm, her left hand instinctively feeling if the hairpins were likely to hold.

"No, I'll no sit doon."

"Are ye afraid?"

"Yes; I dinna like the look o' ye." Then with quick prudential qualification she added, "Ye look so serious."

"So I am serious, Bell — desperate serious. Come, I want to speak to ye."

"But I dinna like serious talk at this time o' day." She flung her arm round the gnarled oak pole of the summer-house and tapped the gravel with the point of her outstretched foot. At this moment remembering her countenance had fallen, she cleared up and added, "When folk are serious, they whiles say disagreeable things; and if you say disagreeable things I'll run away."

"But ye have led me to ettle that what I am going to say will no' be distastefu' to ye."

"Have I? Then I would like to hear it."

Her heart gave a great leap. What was this she had said? Had she actually invited the man to make a proposal? Deliberately she did not mean it, and, indeed, was sorry for it afterwards; but for the moment she could not resist the temptation of being sure of one conquest.

"I want ye to marry me."

Bell laughed an almost hysterical laugh. Here it was at last—her first offer. Her head was in a whirl, and she had to cling to the hard-hearted oak pole for lack of kindlier support. This was the beginning of her victories. But what about the wan face before her? His whole nervous energy was spent in words and feelings. She did not run away, yet he had not strength enough left to embrace her. He had shot for the prize—had he hit or missed the mark?

"I'm awfu' serious," he said. They were both standing limp, and needing mutual succour at the summer-house door.

"I see that," she replied, contemplating the toe of her light shoe; "but I'm owre young." In her heart she was dearly fond of the young man, but the momentary weakness which he had failed to take advantage of was past. She could not throw herself away to the first bidder, nor could she explain that when other offers came she might place him on the short leet.

"You're no' that young," he said.

"Is it fair to remind me of advancing years?" If she had not been at the Edinburgh boarding-school she would not have answered so pertly.

"I didna mean that, Bell; but you are auld enough to be my wife. We have grown up the-gether in a sense."

"That's true; but I'm — I'm barely twenty."

"Is't the siller, Bell — Dr. Congalton's siller that has ta'en ye frae me? If so I wish to God ye had never heard tell o't, for I have enough wi' honest farming to do our turn."

Bell paused; the siller truly had made little difference to her, but she felt it had stirred her mother's desires to set the family on a higher level.

"No, Willie," she said kindly, "it's no' the siller I'm minding about — it makes no odds in my feelings to you; but my mother canna spare me. Na, I wouldna advise ye to ask her." Bell did not wish to lose him absolutely.

"Tell me this," he implored, "has onybody else speired ye?"

"Oh, no." Her vanity returned: she hoped in her heart the next one who came would not ask this embarrassing question. "No one has ever asked me."

"Then ye winna say no to me, Bell?"

"I canna say yes — at present — I would need time."

"What time?" he inquired eagerly — "a month?"

"No, no — a year," she stammered, "at — at — least."

"Let it be a year, then," he said with resignation. "I'll wait."

She was beginning to feel the seriousness of the situation, and was pondering in her mind whether she had done right in being so definite, when her lover, awaking to a sense of what was appropriate, seized her unresisting hand, drew her to him inside the summer-house, and kissed her lips. At the moment she could have returned the kiss warmly, and said, "No, not a year hence, but now." In consonance with the consistency of her sex, however, she struggled from his embrace. The hairpins had held nobly. This was but one — surely there would be other triumphs. Were not these, according to her education, the heritage of well-favoured maidenhood?

"Is it an engagement?" he inquired, contemplating her flushed face, three yards from him now.

"No, no!" she cried, "no engagement on either side. Ask me again in a year, but till then we are both free."

When Richard Cowie and his wife returned from the fair Bell was busy in the kitchen, but her heightened colour and glittering eyes were attributed to the heat of the jam-pan. Willie Mitchell had been prudently instructed to keep out of the way, and show no sign, or she, Bell, would not be answerable for the consequences. Other proposals might come, or, if not, her mother's mind might alter — a year was a long time.

On the Wednesday following there was to be a flower-show at Kilmory, and Mrs. Cowie resolved to be there. She sent her compliments to Mr. Congalton — would he allow his little girl and the governess to accompany her daughter and herself to the show? She knew that an invitation including both would be more likely to find acceptance. It would also have the look of greater disinterestedness, while she and Bell could take stock of this much-talked-of young person, and, if necessary, by their manner at least set her in her place. To Mrs. Cowie's surprise Eva was allowed to accompany her, but the governess was not. Was it a retributive circumstance in the irony of events that this masterful scheming spirit was unconsciously instrumental in taking the child out of the way while the father made a declaration of love, and a proposal of marriage to the lady whom she deliberately designed to humble? The world is too good for such coincidences to occur often, though when we do find a Haman suffering mortal defeat on his own gallows, it would be contrary to our wicked nature to be deeply sorry for him.

Congalton's later life had been a lonely and self-reliant one. The deeper springs of sentiment seemed dried up, or, if they existed, were sealed. For many years solitude had been his

choice, and when drawn into society his asso-
ciates were principally men. The few women
he had met remained entirely outside of his
life — they did not awaken affection. He had
frequently smiled at his brother's Quixotic wish
to will him away in marriage to a farmer's
daughter. What thought had he of marriage?
Yet under his apparently frigid manner there
was, unknown to himself, a spring of latent
passion ready to well forth in response to the
appropriate touch. Since confiding his literary
secret to the governess, that little person had
been an object of enlarging interest to him.
He had created occasions, contrary to his
nature, of being in her society. She was practical, helpful, and never by any means obtrusive.
Her presence brought light and warmth into
his rather sunless life; her necessary absence
awoke the poetry of reminiscence. In fact,
she conquered him without scheme or intention
as she had conquered and won Mistress Izet
and Isaac Kilgour. The result was not of his
seeking, nor of hers. You ask what draws the
bee to the flower, or the swallow to the South —
what answer do you get? Nature is a subtle

worker, and will not be questioned. It was not the outward beauty of face or elegance of form, though the governing influence of mind gave a charm to both. It was the inevitable and irresistible outcome of natural affinity. Did she love him? In very truth she had never thought of him as a lover. She had her ideals, like other women, but Congalton was not one of them. She admired his ability, his power of absorbing, transforming, and ennobling the rude materials with which he worked. He was intensely interested in the occupations of the hour, as all who turn them to lasting account must be; but she felt that existence, in the pauses of his activity, must be dull and monotonous; Eva was too young to bestow the quickening sympathy it lacked. Were her preconceived girlish notions of a lover suffering change? It is impossible to tell the precise moment of time at which the unlikely object or person takes form to fill the ideal niche in the human mind. In her own heart there had sprung up, knowing his needs, an increasing desire to shed something of her own natural brightness on his path. She did not know —

nor did she, in her eager desire to help him, pause to think — that this in itself might be the precursor of a deeper sentiment. The declaration of Congalton's feelings, and the proposal which ensued, while entirely unexpected, revealed to her the true state of her own heart. The occasion was too solemn for laughter. There was no humour in the face of this man, who with his pen could be so daintily humorous. Yet she felt an impulse to laugh — not at him, but at herself. After their day-dreams and their confidences what would her sister Violet think? Did she not already stand among the ruins of her broken gods? Nevertheless, the feeling immediately following was one of joyful acquiescence. For the moment she was oblivious to the future, but only for the moment. No, no, no — it could not be. She was serious now, and had no thought of laughter. Mrs. Maconkey had told her of Dr. Congalton's will. His marriage with her would involve the sacrifice of his interest in it. If that were all — and she was not insensible to its magnitude — she would gladly enter into his life and aid him to retrieve that loss;

but it meant more — it meant also the sacrifice of his daughter's portion: this was insuperable.

It was in vain he assured her that his present means and his capacity for work were ample guarantee that no one should suffer. She felt it was an injustice to the child who was not of age to protect her own interests, and an act to which it would be both dishonest and disloyal on her part to consent.

There was a russet memory of sunset on the shoulder of the Baidland hill as Mrs. Cowie and her daughter took form at the head of the dusky loaning and placed their charge, flushed with the agitation of entertainment, in the kindly arms of Mistress Izet, at Broomfields gate. Neither father nor governess appeared; but Mrs. Cowie derived comfort from the reflection that the child had been much made of, and that she would not be long in reporting to the proper authority the attentions she had received from herself and Bell. Indeed, Eva carried a souvenir of the occasion home with her, for Mrs. Cowie, with the excellent tact for appropriation which distinguished her, laid hands on the bouquet that had carried off the first prize, in order that the child might have in her possession a "minding of the show."

Next morning Hetty announced in the school-room that her pupil was to have some holidays, her father having arranged to take her to the seaside for a change.

"Oh!" cried Eva, clapping her hands with delight, "shall I see the Atlantic Ocean?"

"Yes, my dear, you will see the Atlantic, and the great sands of Machrihanish — won't that be charming?"

"And you will put me on a pony?"

"I fear there are no ponies at Machrihanish; but, Eva dear, I shall not be there. Your father has granted me a few days' leave of absence to visit my own home."

CHAPTER XV

TROUBLE AT BROOMFIELDS

THE smith had got a good story about Farmer Nicol (there was a miller of the same name) which he was relating to the candlemaker between the wicks of the dipping-frame. The sappers and miners were busy in the neighbourhood of Gushetneuk making a survey, and were trespassing freely, and beyond need, without saying by your leave. The farmer, as Pringle said, got "kina nettled," and challenged them, whereupon they showed him "a bit thing ca'd a permit that entitled them, they said, to gang ony gate they liked."

"That wud be a kina leeshins frae the government," said the candlemaker, speaking into his tallow vat.

"Ay, they were michty big aboot it, but wait till ye hear — awa' gaes Gushets and lets oot the bull."

"Gran'!" cried Brough. "Na, but that was richt brawly dune; the bull wudna care a docken for government paper. — Weel?"

"Man, they took to their heels as if the Foul Thief himsel' was efter them."

"And what happened syne?"

"Oh, they cam' roon the back o' the drystane dyke, to the march yett, and keekin' owre, ordered Nicol to tie up the bull. 'Na,' quoth he, quite ceevil and canny-like, 'the beast maun have exercise. I have no right to hinder ye trespassing and neither has the bull, but ye maun satisfee him ye have a permit.'" While the gossips were laughing over Farmer Nicol's strategy, a carriage and pair passed at great speed over the brig, and the candlemaker followed his friend to the door to learn who it might be that was travelling in such unaccustomed haste.

"It's Maister Congalton," cried the smith, having the earlier and the fuller view, ere the horses spanked up the brae. "He has the wee lassie in his arms. I'll wager she's ill; maybe she's got hurt or something."

This surmise was strengthened when, a quarter of an hour later, Isaac Kilgour was seen hurry-

ing across Nanny Welshe's garden as a near cut
for the doctor. Ritchie Kilruth stopped his
work and called after him as he passed; and
Babby Lawson hailed him from her kail-yard,
but the earnestness of his purpose had deafened
him. Isaac had never been seen in such perturbed
haste before. When he had delivered his message he took his way homeward by the loan end,
crossing over the stepping-stones to avoid curiosity. Nevertheless, it was known that evening,
both at Brig-end and at Elsie Craig's well, that
there was fever at Broomfields. To the rustic
mind the name was synonymous with the plague
— not yet having been differentiated. At the
former meeting-place there was genuine alarm,
for some of the older memories could go back to
the cholera, and they had it on the authority of
Kilruth, who had been in foreign parts, "that
some o' thae fevers were that mortal they wud
kill a horse."

Meantime the same carriage which had passed
up during the day with Mr. Congalton and his
daughter, returned in the evening with Miss
Hazlet. The excitement in the household went
down at her presence. Her calm self-possession

and practical ways surprised even the doctor. The case, in medical parlance, was one of scarlet fever, but Hetty had no fear: moreover, she was not without experience, having volunteered to nurse a companion who suffered from the same ailment in the cottage hospital at school.

Congalton spent the afternoon and evening between the sick-room and the study. He had looked on and written about Miss Nightingale in the extemporized hospital at Balaklava, but even she had not filled his mind with greater admiration than he felt for this purposeful and considerate young person in whose presence everything fell into methodical and appropriate order.

When Isaac Kilgour, at Hetty's request, brought up the chair-bed and placed it near that of the patient, Congalton remonstrated, and proposed to engage the services of a nurse from the County Hospital. The remonstrance, however, was in vain. No one knew the temperament of the child as she did — and that was much in such cases. The mother of the maid-of-all-work had tapped at the kitchen window and spirited her daughter away in panic. Hetty knew that the employment of a nurse would simply be adding more trouble to a house already undermanned. Isaac hung about in a kind of anxious daze, courting usefulness; when there was no more to do, he volunteered to help in the kitchen.

During these preliminaries, the patient looked on with flushed cheeks and glistening eyes. Strange thoughts were passing through the ever active mind, but she harboured them till the flurry was over.

" Papa," she whispered, looking in his face with earnest gaze, as he stooped over her to say good-night, " papa, don't people have headaches, or something, before they die? "

" My darling," he replied, with simulated cheerfulness, " why do you think of such things? Miss Hazlet is kindly taking all these precautions to make you well."

" But I have no headache at all, papa; see, I could sit up quite well — my throat is only the least little bit sore — that is all."

Next day the patient was more prostrate physically, but her mind was abnormally active. Memory was undoing her lock-fast places, and flashes of things that had been seemed to fall athwart her mental vision. She was back in the seminary of the "scarlet woman," as Mistress Izet had no hesitation in calling her.

"Oh, Miss Hazlet," Eva opened her eyes as the soft hand of the nurse stole under the clothes seeking the pulse, "you should have seen how angry Miss Vanderbilt was with Flo."

"Flo?"

"Yes, Flo Tregartan, she was the little servant — the kitchen girl, you know — she took pennies out of the young ladies' pockets. Wasn't it naughty to take pennies that were not her own?"

"Yes, dear, it was very naughty; but the doctor says you must try to sleep."

The patient put a hot hand obediently under her cheek and closed her eyes again, but these early school-days had possession of the little brain.

"Flo had a grey laugh," she said, by and by with some degree of mental continuity — "a funny grey laugh, just like a boy's. Miss Vanderbilt had a yellow laugh. Papa's laugh is grey, but different from Flo's. Most of the girls had a white laugh; but none of them had such a nice, sweet, white laugh as yours."

Three days elapsed, and the fever ran its exhausting course. Hetty was with her charge constantly. Mrs. Cowie, honestly anxious about the child's condition, had come in person, and thrown gravel at the kitchen window, receiving the housekeeper's report, with the privet hedge between them.

"Mind and tell the maister I ventured doon bye to speir," she admonished.

The minister did not call, his moral cowardice in the face of infectious trouble was well known, but he charged the doctor not to belittle his anxiety about the patient. The school-master forbade the attendance at school of the kitchen-maid's brother.

"It was sentiment," he explained apologetically to the merchant who kept a limited supply of medicines, "but having the care of youth public sentiment must be respected."

Zedic Lawson complained of a sore throat, and his mouth had a more pronounced exclamatory look ever since the postman returned to tell his wife he had delivered the message to her sister that she was not to call. Only Nancy Beedam would come near the house. She had buried three bairns, and knew what trouble was. On the fourth day, the doctor was not beyond admitting that the case puzzled him.

" Had it not been such a pronounced case of scarlet fever," he said, after a prolonged diagnosis, " I would say the child had measles." True enough, when he next returned measles had developed. A neighbouring practitioner with a long record was summoned for consultation. He had only known one case of the kind in his varied experience. There was a private putting of heads together. Medical science gave measles fourteen days to show itself, and scarlet fever three. On further sifting, it was found to be exactly fourteen days since the flower-show at Kilmory, and measles were known to be rife there. The deduction was inevitable — scarlet fever must have been contracted after the other virus had begun to operate — probably in some highland conveyance or hotel. How beautiful and precise were the deductions of medical science !

Meantime the little sufferer's strength, sorely wounded by the first attack, was but indifferently able to withstand this cruel complication. She suffered from a rasping cough that gave her little rest. Strange thoughts and fancies would come across the patient's mind, finding imperfect expression in broken phrases. At night-time, feeling the needless pang of a tender conscience, she would start up, and kneeling on the bed with her hands and head resting on Hetty's bosom, repeat the little prayer she fancied she had forgotten to say. Though Congalton retired to his room down-stairs after nightfall, it was not to sleep.

These thoughtful vigils revealed to him how tenderly he loved his child. Her quaint sayings and doings, the delightful memory of the intimate companionship of the week they had passed together, haunted him, while overhead on the uncarpeted floor the audible evidence of ministration told of the exhausting sleeplessness of the patient, and the anxious tendance of the nurse. And so this eternity of days and nights rolled slowly on, till the doctor's anxiety became equally divided between the two; the former did not gain strength, and the latter had been by the bedside all the time practically without sleep or rest. Worn at length to submission, Hetty retired, leaving father and child together.

while Mistress Izet kept temporary watch in her own domain, within call. Congalton's masculine and active habits of life had left little time for introspection, but as he sat there, hour after hour, looking at the unnaturally flushed face and swollen lips, between which the light breath passed in fitful pulsations, memory had many backward glances. His wife died when he was on foreign service. The news had broken him for weeks, but he had been spared the sight of her suffering, and the pain of articulate fare-wells. In his daughter he had recently seen, at unexpected moments, startling glimpses of resemblance to her mother. In smile, in glance, in gesture, in the sudden pose of her head. Poor Eve, as he loved playfully to call her, pain-worn and fever-tossed, how his heart melted in tender desire — what suffering would he not have endured if suffering were vicarious? It is at such moments strong men pray, in their utter helplessness. Towards midnight the patient became uneasy; the parched lips moved as the little head turned in the golden sheen of her hair. He stooped reverently, to catch the half-uttered words —

"Jesus . . . tender . . . Shepherd, hear me . . ."

Her lips still moved, but there was only the sound of lisping breath; with an access of earnest entreaty, however, she continued more audibly —

"Through . . . the . . . darkness . . . be Thou . . . near me . . ."

Tears came to this strong man's eyes as his own heart went from him in fervent supplication for the fulfilment of the child's prayer. Congalton was not a praying man, and he was heathen enough not to know the little prayer Eva had been taught to utter devoutly at Hetty's knee; the appropriate simplicity and pathos of the words, however, struck him. The "little lamb," unconscious of his presence, was calling out of the darkness for succour. He took her small burning hands in his, and held them soothingly, but even in this intense wish to be near and help his own child, he felt how helplessly far he was removed from her — the fevered head still continued restless, and the dry lips moved with the sibilant lispings of inarticulate words. Congalton had seen the furious surge of battle; the thinning of solid ranks, the brilliant charge at the cannon's mouth, with comrades and acquaintances falling all around, but the blood was coursing in militant madness, imagination and reflection had no nook in which to brood. Nothing in the red front of war was ever half so unmanning to the paternal heart as the fevered restlessness of his suffering child. While he watched, and compassionated, Eva opened her eyes: they glittered for a moment, but not with recognition.

"Miss Hazlet, Miss Hazlet, is it a long way to the Happy Land? — see — I forgot to say my prayers."

She started to her knees, but he took her in his arms and tried tenderly to control her.

"My darling, my darling," he whispered in her ear, "you have said your prayers already," but she did not regard his words. Putting her finger-tips reverently together, she rested her hands on his shoulder, while he pressed her gently to his breast. He could not mistake the burning, but imperfectly lisped words now —

"Jesus — tender Shepherd — hear me,
    Bless — thy little lamb — to-night,
    Through the darkness — be Thou near me,
    Keep me safe till morning light. — God bless papa . . "

Her over-exerted strength had collapsed — but she had prayed for herself and — for him. It was the last supreme effort. He laid her down tenderly, and was smoothing her head on the pillow, when Hetty stole noiselessly into the room and slipped to his side. The breathing was not so laboured now. Hetty stooped to listen. It was no time for womanly tears. She raised her head without looking in his face, and murmured a few words brokenly.

.   .   .   .

He did not answer. He stooped and kissed the small, pale brow that had lately pressed his shoulder. " My poor Eve!"

" God's Eve," was the amended response.

CHAPTER XVI

HETTY HAZLET AT HOME

IT was five weeks, luckily, before Barbara Lawson would allow her sister, Mistress Izet, to enter her door. Even then she conversed with her over the kitchen table. Though Zedie knew of his sister-in-law's visit, he kept eidently to his loom. Mistress Izet had sat in his chair, and the poor man thought so much about it that he took catarrh in the head, and on the third day a rash appeared on his chest. The smith, who had some skill of ordinary troubles, said it was "fancy, complicated wi' thinness o' bluid," and ordered him some "openin' medicine." The kitchen-girl had returned to do "orra jobs" at Broomfields, but slept at home. Mrs. Cowie regarded the recent dispensation very much in the light of how it would bear upon her own plans. She felt the death of the child swelled the total of her daughter's tocher, but it had minimized the chances of an alliance which would have soothed her ambition and made her practically mistress of the whole. The library had not done much for her, but as yet the chances had been against it, owing to the "smittal" trouble in Broomfields. On this subject she was angered by William Lonen, the school-master. William was not a humourist, nor was he a lover of light literature, but he laughed right out when he glanced at the miscellaneous collection of antiquated and obsolete tomes, and with the brutality of a man not accustomed to respect feelings, said they would be handy on the counter for small parcels if she ever started shopkeeping. To do her justice, whatever her motives were, Mrs. Cowie was the first to visit Broomfields to offer sympathy.

"Na, but ye set thae mourning things brawly," her husband had remarked, coming in hot from the harvest-field as his wife was preparing to depart. "Will ye say onything anent the wee thing's siller?"

"It'll depend on hoo the crack turns," she replied, looking in the glass for justification of her husband's compliment. Compliments were not rife with him.

Congalton was neither blind nor deaf to Mrs. Cowie's shallow pretensions. The conversation did not turn as was desired, and she could not force confidence, though she tried bravely. As a result of her interview, it was somehow, though not without resistance, borne in on her mind that he would never marry Bell.

Her visit to Broomfields was so barren in everything, even in news, that she halted at the school-house to have a gossip with Mrs. Lonen. There she learned that the governess had returned to her own home. The minister had told the school-master, and the school-master confided to his wife, that the young doctor was fair off his head about the little woman who had nursed his patient.

"The sly piece! She kens fine hoo to set her feathers for the men."

"Na, but they tell me she was by-ord'nar at the nursing."

"May be that," said Mrs. Cowie dryly; "but the wean dee't; there's no muckle to show for guid nursing. I suppose the maister packed her aff when her work was dune. I'm thinking he'd have been better ser't wi' a proper nurse from the first."

"As to packing her off, I'm no clear about that. Mistress Izet is said to alloo that either the doctor or Mr. Congalton will marry her."

"Mr. Congalton!" cried Mrs. Cowie.

"Ay, or the doctor, she doesna ken which o' the twa's daftest aboot her."

On her way home Mrs. Cowie forgathered with Nanny Pinkerton, the spae-wife. On ordinary occasions she would have given this woman the go-bye, but disappointment had provoked impatience. She invited her civilly to tea, if peradventure spae-craft might be able to forecast some glimpse of the future. It was a pitiful pass to which this strong-willed woman had come, but she knew that neither Bell nor her husband would be at home to see it. The sibyl tossed her cup and plied her art according to custom, but by her own confession only groped in the dark.

The revelation she had to make was all about the sea. Nan cast the cup many times with similar results. The marine disaster, repeatedly foretold, was tantalizingly irrelevant to the situation, and afforded Mrs. Cowie but small portent of good. Her brother-in-law was a sea-faring man — the captain of a sailing vessel, with a wife and four small children, living from hand to mouth in Saltcoats. The women, however, had not exchanged words since the funeral of Mrs. Cowie senior. The old lady lived and died in the house of her daughter-in-law in the seaport town, and naturally left all she possessed to her. There was not much to differ about, but Mrs. Cowie said the old lady had promised her silver spoons to Bell, and threatened to break the will. That night there were high words, needlessly, at Windy-yett, after Bell and the servants retired to bed. Mrs. Cowie had brooded all afternoon and evening over the spae-woman's forecast, and at length settled down to the unwavering conviction that disaster had overtaken Captain Cowie, and that somehow the legal burden of those dependent on him would fall on her and her husband. The farmer could not understand his wife's sudden and unexpected interest in the captain and his affairs. She put many leading questions, and elicited that her brother-in-law was on his way home from Jamaica to the Clyde.

"If onything happened till him, wud the law throw the burden o' his wife and weans on us?"

"But what puts it into your head that onything has happened? Have ye heard ill news?"

"I'm just speirin'," she said curtly.

"Speirin'," he replied, with uncommon heat; "you're just blethering like a young canary."

Had her wedded husband been a wool-broker, as might have been, Mrs. Cowie felt she would not have been treated with such indignity.

"As to the law," her husband continued, "I kenna what it could mak' us do; but if onything happens to Jack, I suppose we couldna stand by and see them withoot bite and sup, so lang as we had it to spare."

"Ay, ye'll bring them in and set them doon i' the best corner o' the house without speirin' leave, I suppose."

"Wha has asked ye to tak' them in?" cried Windy-yett, in a higher tone than was natural to him. This subject was a tinder-box which had often been ignited before, and was therefore easily kindled. "You're surely running aff wi' the harrows a' thegether."

"Ye've said enough," she replied firmly. "I ken your mind, Ritchie Cowie, but let me tell ye this, if ever Nancy Cowie or ane o' hers enters this door to bide — then guid-bye to ye."

She snapped her fingers in a passion, and went off to bed. For the moment Congalton and his concerns, as well as her own matrimonial schemes, were out of mind. The reading of the cups had brought no comfort. Those who, perforce, would compel prevision, will, as like as not, miss their immediate aim, and probably, as in this case, find that revealed to them which it is not for their peace of mind to know.

Meantime the call for Hetty Hazlet at Broomfields had come to an end. She had fought and prayed for the life of the child, but all had been in vain. She resolved to give no occasion for speculation as to the relationship between Mr. Congalton and herself by lingering under his roof when her work was done. How dreadfully strange and mysterious that the child in whose interests she had declined to marry Mr. Congalton should be so suddenly removed. This thought was on the mind of both at parting, but the grief was so fresh and overmastering that neither dared to touch it.

Hetty enjoyed the rest at home among her own people. Her sojourn at Kilspindie had ripened and broadened her mind in many ways, but it had told on her health. Autumn was at its best in fruit and colour. The parish of Kilbaan was then, and is reputed to be still, one of the best-wooded districts in Ayrshire. The over-ripe woods in Balgrey Glen, and along the valley of the Arne to where it issues from Loch Sheen, seemed as if they had burst into flame of various degrees of intensity. With her absorbing love of nature, it was delightful to roam alone among the woods in the first days of her freedom, and in her communings with the soothing objects around, to exclude from her mind the scenes which overclouded the immediate retrospect. As a child she knew these age-worn and mouldy paths, now noisy to the feet by reason of the heavy pile of the varied leaf-carpet which a couple of nips of frost had laid for her. To these woods her father used to conduct her in spring and teach her, as far as he himself knew it, the mystery of bursting bud and uncurling frond. Later, she would steal out by herself, this timid little girl, with the wide, inquiring eyes, and watch this object-lesson, while the wild hyacinth developed a cerulean sheen above the young grass, and primroses like golden stars twinkled in bosky places. Then, ere she knew, soft yellow whorls would appear on the chestnut; and the great pillared glen, cut off from the sun by its ample happing of leaves, would drowse in the insect hum of summer. But when the robin piped among the mellowing fruit on the ancient pear-tree, and blood-red foils spotted the decaying green of the hedge round the manse garden, it was then her pulses tingled with delight, for she knew the brown nuts were on the hazels, the red rowans on the mountain-ash, and that the woods were aglow with transforming colour. These and other memories recurred to her during these meditative rambles. There were also visits to pay to old friends in bien farm towns, whose hospitality, always hearty, was broadened by an abundant harvest early and safely gathered.

Miss Hazlet often accompanied Hetty in her excursions. It was a really happy time for both girls, for they had mutual confidences to exchange in the quiet loanings. The young minister, Mr. Breckenridge, their father's successor, had proposed to Miss Hazlet since Hetty and her sister last met. They were engaged, but the engagement had not yet been formally announced. There was to be a sale of work for repairs on the manse, and the ladies young and old in this and the neighbouring parishes were working for it with might and main, and such news prematurely spread would have been detrimental to this laudable energy — they were pawky, these worldly lovers. Even Andra Carruthers, the beadle, who knew most of the manse secrets, had to be kept in ignorance of this one. The beadle was at first rather jealous of the sudden activity of the congregation under the new minister, but he was not slow to put the proper appraisement upon it.

"Wait," he said to Hetty one day, when they were talking over church matters, "wait till the minister marries — it'll mak' a lock o' difference. He may add ae willing worker to the manse, but my certie, there'll be a heap fewer workers i' the congregation."

Being great friends, Hetty gently sounded this mighty official as to his opinion of her father's successor as a preacher.

"Weel, ye see, Miss Hetty, a buddy that's no bigoted comes roun'. At first, I confess to ye, I was sair exerceest. He writes every word o' his sermons, but it wasna a' thegether that. I dare say ye'll have heard tell o' the day when he tauld us that Heaven wi' its golden streets, and its pearly gates, and Hell wi' its fire and brimstane, were mere feegurs o' speech intended, so to speak, for carnal minds. That as gold and pearls were precious things, and much to be desired, so fire and brimstone were commodities, as it were, folk would keep faurest awa' frae. That in their leeteral sense these things were monstrous conceptions o' Heaven and Hell. Weel, as sure as death, Miss Hetty, I was mortal shocked. Thinks I to mysel', this is awfu'. Is it my duty to carry the books to a man that's spoilin' the profession for baith o' us by rakin' the very hert oot o' — the bad place. Miss Hetty, I'm just telling ye the honest truth hoo I felt. I did not ken what wye to look, till my e'e fell on the face o' Saunders M'Phee, i' the front o' the laft. Ye ken the wye Saunders has o' aye nod, noddin' when a thing pleases him? Weel, I didna see him noddin', but there was a bit smile at the corners o' his lips that maistly follows his nods when he's satisfeet. Thinks I, I'll do nothing rash till I've seen Saunders. It'll maybe be a Presbytery business: they can easily send

anither minister, but whare would they get a
beadle? — no in this parish. So, efter denner,
I daunners alang to the schulehoose, and meets
Saunders at the door. 'Weel,' says I, 'what
do ye think o' your minister noo?' Saunders
was great on him. 'Better and better,' says
Saunders. 'That was a grand discourse we
had the day.' 'But did ye hear what he said
aboot Heaven and — the ither place?' says
I, thinking maybe the bit had slipped him.
'Man, he spoke oot weel at yon bit,' quoth
Saunders, 'we maun get rid o' thae auld mate-
rialistic notions.' 'Ye were on the wye to be a
minister yoursel',' says I — for it was because o'
this I lippened till him. 'True,' quoth he, 'that
was lang syne; but I didna go foret, for I never
could have dared to preach what I believed —
they would have deposed me. Yet my views
were then, what Mr. Breckenridge and other
spiritually-minded ministers are preaching the
day. Be thankfu' for this, and dinna vex yoursel',' he says kindly. 'In my young days I was
taught that the devil was placed i' the world to
tempt us to evil, while God was represented as
standing owre us ready to detect and punish

sin, and, being a thochtfu' callant, between the twa I had a mortal bad time o't. The tender and protecting fatherhood of the Almighty as revealed in His Son had no place in the auld theology. I tell ye, Sandy, I had no peace till I coupet the cairt, gied up John Calvin, and took to reading the Scriptures for mysel' wi' an open mind.' 'But dinna ye believe in fire and brimstane?' quoth I, laith to let the thing slip. 'No,' says he, 'I believe in an intellectual hell. Wrang-doing i' the end will have the same effect on mind and conscience as fire and brimstane has on the body.'"

"I have often thought Saunders should write a book," said Hetty.

"For mercy sake, dinna put that into his head. I ance heard o' a minister wha did that, but he wrote himsel' inside oot and then he was dune. It's a comfort hearing Saunders coming oot by degrees — being mysel' a man o' the auld schule, so to speak, he has helpet me owre a guid wheen prejudices — I am beginning to understan' the minister better. Sam'l Filshie thinks him owre broad, but broad or no broad, he has brocht a heap o' folk to the kirk that never darkened the door afore — no disrespect, Miss Hetty, to your worthy faither. Jeems Warnock, the freethinker, Willie Whammond, the chartist, Dougie Brand, and ithers I could name, have now sittings, and what is mair, pay for them. Speaking o' that puts me in mind o' a guid story. Ye mind Habbie Steenston, the twister, Miss Hetty? Weel, Habbie was twa hauf years ahin-haun wi' his seat-rent. Habbie would cheat even the kirk if he could get aff wi't. So I tells the minister. 'Oh, ask him to speak to me in the vestry,' says he, taking aff his gown. So my man comes in, turning his bonnet round and round unco sheepish like, wi' ae ee looking stracht oot o' the window, and the other fixed o' the airm o' the minister's chair —ye mind hoo Habbie glee't? Aweel, but he aye glee't waur when he was excited. 'I'm glad to see you and the mistress so regular in your places on the Sabbath day,' says the minister, 'but they tell me you get behind wi' the seat-rent.' 'Ay,' says Habbie, 'twisting's gey bad the noo' — that was a story, but the man was never a great hand at the truth. 'Ye smoke?' says the minister. 'Ou-ay, I smoke,' quoth

Habbie. 'How much will ye smoke in the week?' 'I never took thocht; it's the wife buys the tobacco.' 'Will you smoke a couple of ounces?' says the minister, pegging at him hard. 'Like enough,' says the man. 'Weel,' quoth the minister, 'most of us have to make sacrifices, suppose you knock an ounce a week off your smoking — and pay your seat-rents.' 'But ye forget, sir,' quoth Habbie quite innocently, 'ye forget I get some guid o' my smokin'.' Miss Hetty, ye could have tied the minister wi' a straw, as the sayin' is. He tauld the story right hertily efter-hin to Saunders M'Phee, though it was against himsel'. The minister thocht the twister was a humourist; but when I spoke to Habbie gaun up the Ell brae on the Monday, he seemed to think he had the worst o' the crack, especially when the minister laughed at him; in truth he was on his wye owre to the cork to borrow money to pay his seats."

Hetty entertained the little home-circle afterwards with the beadle's stories. As a brother-in-law she felt satisfied Mr. Breckenridge would do.

CHAPTER XVII

A CHAPTER OF ACCIDENTS

CHRISTMAS dawned, if such could be truly said about it, to find ditches obliterated, and all minor irregularities on the face of the landscape brought to a common level. During the previous day and night the air had been weighted with a dense mist of snow thick as dust in a sunbeam. The houses on the west side of the long street which contained the bulk of the population of Kilbaan being open to the drift, were snowed up, most of them above the horizontal bar of the half-door. All outside labour in forest and field was arrested, but there was ample employment at home. Man, woman, and child, capable of wielding spade or shovel, had been busy from early morn liberating themselves or their neighbours from the white drift that blocked windows and doors. It was twelve o'clock before the last prisoner was free. But a fresh excitement was kindled in the village mind when the beadle came ploughing along the lee-side of the road, driving the dry snow from his knees, shouting and gesticulating. The men were standing upright resting on the implements they had been using, in the spaces they had cleared; women and children, eased in their minds as to their own personal safety, hurried to the door at this new note of alarm.

" It's a tragedy," said the drainer, shading his eyes to survey the approaching figure.

" Od, I'll no say but the mail-coach is coupet," Sam'l Filshie remarked, forcing definiteness into Whammond's exclamation.

" I had a terrible dream," Mrs. Warnock came out to the middle of the road to say — she had lost her temper in the kirk the day before because her man had not joined in the singing of the last Psalm; but no one had patience to listen to her dream with the beadle yelling — " Come on wi' your spades fast, lads, or Maister Breckenridge will be smoored."

Seeing he was understood Carruthers turned

and retraced his steps as fast as such an im-
possibility could be performed, followed by a
miscellaneous band of armed workers headed
by Jeems Warnock and Willie Whammond.
How the minister had got into this trouble
puzzled them much. The manse stood high,
and was protected on the windward side by a
mound of fir-trees. Such snow as had whirled
past to the garden wall, had been mostly dissi-
pated by the high wind of the early morning,
so that the manse itself suffered little.

After an early breakfast the minister, from an
upper window, looked out over the village to
see how it fared with his flock — they were busy,
he saw, helping one another, which was true
Christian work. But while watching their
activity, there was another house to which his
mind naturally reverted, less safe, because more
isolated and exposed, and that was the small
homestead at the parish march occupied by his
predecessor. As Providence allowed it, at that
moment he saw the head of his trusty beadle
rising above the stile on the east wall of the
glebe.

Carruthers had been busy all morning cutting

an outlet from his own door, and it was only
after the job was done that he thought of his
late master and his helpless family of women
folk. By the time the beadle reached the manse
the minister had girded on his leggings, and in
a few minutes the former, armed with a spade,
and the latter with a shovel, were hurrying along
to the parish march on their mission of mercy.
They kept the lown side of the road, which was
protected by a matted hedge. On the other
side snow was piled against an embankment as
high as the kirk gable. The plantation on the
right, so well known to them, was storm-beaten
almost out of recognition. During the night
the wind and snow had pelted the trees till the
upright poles assumed enormous girth, one part
wood and three parts snow. How this mysterious element had transformed the landscape!
All familiar landmarks were obliterated — dykes,
hedges, burns were muffled and undistinguish-
able. Even the loch, with its fringe of reeds
and seggans, was swallowed up in the prevailing
whiteness. At an intersecting loaning a great
bar of soft snow had got impounded while the
conflicting currents fought for supremacy.

When they had cut their way through this barrier and reached the turning of the road, the minister gave a sudden whistle of exclamation. The cottage in which the aged minister and his family lived was situated in a hollow, below the level of the turnpike road, which modern engineering skill had made up to save gradients. The space between the road and the front of the cottage was entirely filled, the snow-wave not seeking pause till it climbed half-way up the roof. It was probably this sight that perturbed the minister and made him incautious, for, taking a false, and as it seemed to the beadle, a fatal step, he stumbled over the embankment and disappeared in the devouring abyss beneath.

This was the occasion of the beadle's lamentable outcry for succour. It was not long till willing helpers were on the scene. The first thing that Sam'l Filshie did was to fall down the slope himself, taking the drainer, whose sleeve was within reach, along with him. Andra Carruthers, though overwhelmed at the moment by this additional mishap, declared, when the upshot was known, that it " wis a perfect providence o' the Almichty." The descent of the two men made a considerable opening in the snow-wreath. Moreover, they tumbled on the top of the minister, who, overcome by cold, lay unconscious at the bottom. Agitated by so much healthy and militant life, the yielding element soon gave way, and left Filshie and Whammont space to breathe. They lifted the minister between them till his head was above the snow; the shock he had received by their fall, and the subsequent handling combined with the keen fresh air soon restored consciousness, and enabled him to stand on his own feet.

When the alarm was first raised that the minister was smoored, Davit Winterbottom the joiner, who was reckoned the best man in the parish at drawing an inference, jaloused, as he said to Filshie on the way back, that Maister Breckenridge had fan doon the Minister's Brae; and if so a leather micht be a serviceable thing. So just as the young minister's head came above the snow for fresh air, Davit and his apprentice appeared at the bend of the road, carrying the ladder between them. The opportuneness of this sight was recognized by a cheer from those who stood by communing with themselves as to how the men were to get out. In a few minutes by the aid of the ladder the imprisoned trio stood on the road among their neighbours, little the worse of their immersion. Meantime the villagers without pause attacked the unresisting snow with such weapons as they had at hand.

While this work was going forward, the minister had time to reconnoitre and think. At one end of the cottage roof a thin wreath of smoke began to ascend languidly. He had remarked on the absence of smoke a moment before the accident.

"They are taking hert, sir, and mending the fire," said the beadle; "no doubt they will hear by this time that we are trying to howk them out."

The question of hearing was seriously troubling the minister; they probably had heard too much. He was afraid that the alarm as to his own personal safety might have been heard by them; his voice no doubt could reach and reassure them if he spoke loud enough, but the thought of shouting to the empty air bordered on comedy.

"Would ye like to speir if they're a' richt

inside?" inquired Winterbottom, with the ladder on his shoulder.

"The very idea that was on my mind; but how is it to be done?"

"Oh, easy."

The joiner was a man of resource. In a couple of minutes, by the aid of the ladder, he had bridged the gleaming gulf, and was speaking down one of the smokeless chimneys. It was some time before the ghostly voice reached the inmates, who were, at the moment, gathered together round the kitchen fire for warmth.

"Are they all safe?" Mr. Breckenridge had a lover's impatience.

"I havena reached them yet."

"Call louder, they——" the minister did not proceed, for he saw from the attitude of his friend's head that he was listening.

"They're a' richt, sir, but they've been mortal anxious about yoursel'——they heard the beadle's cries when ye tumelt owre the bank."

"Who is answering you?"

"Miss Hazlet."

"All right; if you come down and hold the ladder, I will go up and speak to her."

The household had never had serious anxiety for their own safety, but, as the joiner reported, they were greatly alarmed about the accident which they knew had befallen the minister. Winterbottom's stentorian voice had assured them of his safety, and Hetty returned to the kitchen to convey the news to her parents, leaving her sister to listen by the fireplace.

"Violet!" She started. Could it be? — yes, it was Mr. Breckenridge's voice. The name was repeated more audibly.

"I am here. Oh, Will, take care; are you much hurt?"

"Not at all hurt."

"Are you there alone?"

"Yes, the joiner is at the other end of the ladder. Are you all comfortable inside?"

"Quite comfortable, thank you. Oh, Will dear, it is so kind of you — Here's Hetty, she thinks it so awfully good of you and the neighbours."

"Are you in utter darkness?"

"Oh, no, the upper half of the back windows are clear of snow."

"Now that we know you are all safe and

in comparative comfort the situation dawns upon me as rather funny ; don't you think so ? "

The vibration of a soft musical laugh ascended the chimney. Was it Hetty's?

Miss Hazlet, with a smile in her reply, admitted that it was " certainly a little odd."

" Advise him to get down," whispered Hetty, " the minister sitting on the rigging — it is too ridiculous."

The picture to the imagination of the girls was more grotesque than it appeared to the sense of the busy workers outside.

"Shall I speak, Violet, and tell him to get down ? "

" No, please don't," Violet pleaded, holding her sister back. " Think, he has risked his life for us. He would be offended if he suspected we were laughing at him. Will?"

" Yes."

" Do you think it will take long to reach us?"

" Perhaps an hour, the drift has been frightful. — A moment —" he said, and they heard his voice travelling through the clear, thin air to some one at a distance. " It is the post-lad from Muirtown," he resumed. " The poor fellow has made a most heroic struggle. The post-cart was utterly useless; he has taken five hours to get over the three miles. There is a letter for Miss Hetty. Shall I take delivery of it ?"

" Yes, please."

There was a pause during which the sisters speculated as to who the unexpected correspondent might be.

" Violet," from the chimney-top.

" Yes, Will."

" Is Miss Hetty there?"

" Yes."

" I've got the letter; it is in a literary hand, and bears the London post-mark. Shall I open it and deliver its contents *viva voce* down the chimney ?"

Miss Hazlet clapped her hands and laughed. It was rare of Will to make such good fun for them in this odd situation.

" Please don't," cried Hetty, looking up and seeing a good-natured smiling face framed in the circle above. " The chimney is quite wide — look, I can see you. It will be perfectly safe to drop it down."

" You will not blame me if it miscarries ? "

" There is no fear of that."

" It may be very important."

" I will risk it."

The ridiculousness of the situation was not so apparent to Hetty now. The letter crunkled down the chimney and fell at her feet — she recognized the hand. Hetty ran off to her bedroom, where shortly afterwards Violet found her sitting alone. There was a happy light in her eyes, but the face was thoughtful.

" Hetty, dear, have you good news ? Who is your correspondent? "

Hetty handed her the letter in reply, her eyes the while unconsciously reading her sister's face. Miss Hazlet read the first sentence, then, woman-like, turned to the signature —

" Mr. Congalton ! " she exclaimed, and the sunshine brightened in her features as she read on. " Hetty, he is coming to renew his offer of marriage, and to ask papa to let you be his wife." Violet laid down the letter, took the little sister in her arms, and kissed her with true feeling. Hetty averted her face to hide the starting tears. " Do you not love him, dear? "

"Oh, Violet, after what I have told you, how can you ask? It is not that."

"I know," said Miss Hazlet sympathetically; "but it is different for him now, and he is so lonely."

"There is still the will."

"Oh, bother that absurd will! Is Mr. Congalton to remain unmarried all his life, or marry some one he cannot love because of a stupid, capricious will? Has he not already told you he is independent of his brother's money? You do not treat him fairly, Hetty."

"Do you think so, Violet? I only thought of him. You do not know how good and clever he is — and, oh, how unselfish."

"Then give him the reward he desires; he is worthy of it, according to your own showing. Let me see —," Violet took up the letter again. "He expects to be here by the 24th or 25th at latest. The letter has been detained. Hetty, he may be here to-day."

Miss Hazlet returned with a light step to the kitchen, and broke the happy news to her parents.

The aged minister and his wife had had a

long and, on the whole, a happy journey together. Their respect for and confidence in
each other had never wavered. In all questions
of interest affecting his daughters you might
expect the father to say, " Well, have you
spoken to your mother — she is always right ? "
While the maternal reply would run on similar
lines—" You know I never decide anything without consulting your father, he is so wise." Now
that they were both frail and reduced to limited
means, their prevailing anxiety naturally was
for the future of their girls. It is but truth to
say that an intense feeling of gratitude filled
their hearts as they saw a way opened up in
the darkness to comfort and happiness for both.
The mother sought Hetty in her room.

Few words were needed to reveal the condition of her daughter's heart: there are other
ways than speech known to women in expressing sympathy. They held each other in
the grasp of affection till arrested by a loud
knocking at the outer door, which was opened
by a frail, white-haired man in ministerial garb.

The good-hearted neighbours, their work done,
stood respectfully on the gleaming road, with

the implements of deliverance on their shoulders, ready to depart. In tones tremulous with emotion Dr. Hazlet thanked them for their timely deliverance. Then turning to his successor he shook his hand warmly. Behind the young minister, however, there was a stranger who was not personally known to the elder man, waiting for admission to the little family circle. Congalton had come on the scene under unconventional and romantic circumstances. The letter had been much retarded by the snow, but not the lover.

CHAPTER XVIII

ISAAC KILGOUR ARRIVES AT A DECISION

CONGALTON'S visit to Kilbaan was necessarily brief, but Hetty's confession to her mother and sister procured for him a cordial reception, and rendered his mission an easy and successful one. There was great political disquietude in Peru, with the immediate prospect of serious trouble, for the Spanish Government, taking advantage of a quarrel between some Basque emigrants and the natives, in which many lives were lost, took forcible possession of the Chincha Islands, and Congalton was commissioned by the *Despatch* to proceed at once to the scene of action in the interests of that enterprising newspaper. It was arranged that his marriage with Hetty should take place on his return. In prospect of this new relationship his affairs had to be recast and put in legal order. A visit to Mr. Sibbald and a formal meeting with his brother's trustees effected this. Broomfields was to be sold or let; and as he would now have to live entirely by his profession, it was necessary that he and his wife should reside in London. It was not without a secret pang of regret that Hetty acquiesced in this proposed separation of herself from her family and the scenes and friends of her early years, but that she felt was nothing in the balance against the sacrifice he was making for her. These important matters settled, Congalton bade an affectionate good-bye to the little household, and set forth with a light heart and fresh hopes on his eventful mission.

Snow and frost with iron grip held undisputed possession of hill and vale, loch and stream, till the last week in February. There had not been such a severe and lasting winter within living memory. Between dozing in his chair and reading such literature as fell within his reach, consisting of odd volumes of Tait's *Edinburgh Magazine*, Herdman's *Guide to Horticulture*, seasoned by an old book of sermons, Isaac Kilgour crept through a somewhat somnolent and enervating season. He was aware that the master had gone abroad, and that Broomfields was in the market. This information had been conveyed to him and Mistress Izet by the same post. They were also informed that Mr. Congalton had provided a small annual pension for each of them, to be remitted in quarterly payments during his lifetime. Meantime they were to remain at Broomfields as heretofore, keeping the house and garden in order till the property passed to other hands. Isaac had a dreamy notion in his mind that something would have to be done in the ordering of his own affairs, but as the place was not yet actually sold there was time to dream and drift.

With the advent of March the snow disappeared before the influence of balmy winds and gentle rain. The fearless snowdrop wagged a defiant head, and the crocus cleft the moist earth and opened its gleaming petals in response to the gracious but tardy smile of spring. Exercise was beginning to lubricate the joints and remove the numbness which long inaction had produced in Isaac's limbs. All morning he had been digging and pottering about the rhubarb roots with a vague feeling of apprehension on his mind. About ten o'clock he paused with a foot on the shoulder of the spade which he was about to strike into the loamy earth. His dull eye seemed riveted on the garden hedge, where a knitted tracery of stems and branches sparkled at every joint with luminous buds of rain. He was not considering this poetic aspect of nature; his activity was arrested by hearing rather than by sight. It was the approaching jog of the carrier's cart in the ruts, and the masterful "hap-back then" of the carrier himself that caught his ear. This useful functionary had made an early start that morning from the county town, where, the day before, Broomfields, according to advertisement, was to be exposed for sale. Isaac waited with his foot on the spade till the carrier was on the other side of the hedge, then he coughed. He did not wish to show his feelings, and if there was bad news — if the place was really sold, it might be as well that he should hear the tidings while he himself was out of view.

"Is that you, Isaac?"

"Umph'm."

"Come to the yett, I have news for ye."

" No, I dinna want Janet to hear, cry't owre."

The horse did not pause, but McLennan's form darkened the network of branches, and gave opaqueness to the gems.

" Broomfields was knocket doon at the roup."

" Wha till?"

" Some lawyer body, they tell me."

" Umph'm."

This was all the news Isaac wanted, and the colloquy ended. The gardener resumed his digging with furious energy. The candle-maker made boast that his ideas flowed fastest in the kirk, during sermon time, but Isaac's were always most active when he was hard at work. Two hours later, when Mistress Izet came to call him to dinner, there was a bead of perspiration on the point of his nose, and a rim of shifting moisture under his chin. She had been cooking the dinner, and did not know what had perturbed him.

" Eh, Isaac," she remonstrated, " ye'll be having the rheumatics again, slaving yersel' that gate. Somebody may buy the place that'll no thenk ye for yer pains. I declare ye mind me o' a wumman in Houston parish —— "

But Isaac was in no mood to hear about the additional foolishness of this old friend in Houston parish, to whom he was supposed to bear some resemblance. He plunged the spade into the soft earth, took out his red pocket-handkerchief, mopped away the perspiration, and went up the stair for dinner. Even the parrot noticed that he had a disturbed mind, and urged him in tones that seemed to imply genuine desire to "let the bruit awa'."

He ate his lonely meal mechanically, changed his boots, put on his blue Kilmarnock bonnet, and slipped quietly out by the back gate. There was a loaning skirting the plantain which led down through the holm to the river. Isaac took this path, crossed the stream on the stepping-stones, and ascended the brae on the other side, leading to the manse. About half-way up this brae, on the left, there was a small deserted house with a few square yards of garden ground in front. This space was protected by a low beech hedge, to which last year's leaves still clung, whispering expressions of hopefulness to the timid March buds. Isaac paused, and looked long and wistfully at the place. The door was weather-beaten, and had not made acquaintance with paint for many a day. There was one red chimney can at the apex of the gable, but the irregular embrasures round the top showed that it had been a tempting target for the school-boys in their destructive leisure. Some of the missiles had evidently missed the higher mark, but had not altogether been thrown in vain, as the glass and astragals of the window plainly set forth. The garden plot was frouzy and fetid with decayed vegetation. There was no need to push open the gate — the hinges, wearied and worn by the irritating and unchecked antics of the wind, had at last dropped it to rot amongst the mouldy undergrowth. Although Isaac knew the place well, he stepped up to the window and looked in. It was a single apartment, with an earthen floor. There was a large open fire-place with a good hobbed grate, a dresser and a cosy set-in bed. The gardener had spent many a couthie gloaming hour at that fire end, while Betty Inglis was in life. Betty held the tenure of this house (being on glebe ground) in virtue of her services to the parish. She assisted the beadle

243

in the menial work of keeping the kirk in order. This duty had originally devolved on his sister, but having married a tailor she felt above such servitude.

For many years Isaac's matrimonial thoughts, so far as he gave them play, swayed between Betty Inglis and Janet Izet. Bet was a rattling talker, and said indiscreet, albeit entertaining things. Her notions of hospitality were talk — continuous talk. To Isaac, who did little to lighten the monologue she was "gran' company," when the leisure of the evening led him across the stepping-stones. Betty, however, was at rest up yonder on the other side of the kirkyard wall, and her humble abode was now tenantless.

The gardener heaved a sigh, and stepped up the brae towards the manse. The doctor was just leaving as he reached the door. The minister received Isaac kindly; he had heard that Broomfields was about to pass into other hands, and was honestly sorry for this lone and taciturn man.

"I suppose you have come to tell me the news about the sale," said Mr. Maconkey, leading the way into the study, and setting a seat for his visitor. 244

"Pairtly," said Isaac.

"It is the doctor who has bought the place; he has just called to tell me he gave his agent instructions to attend the roup and bid for it. I am truly grieved for you and Mistress Izet at having to leave such a comfortable home. The doctor tells me he will require your apartment for his own coachman, but as his man is a poor hand at garden-work, he may be able to give you employment now and then. I understand Mr. Congalton has generously given you both a small allowance to eke out a livelihood. Mistress Izet will repair to her sister's till she gets a place, I suppose?"

"Maybe," said Isaac curtly.

"As for you, perhaps I could find you a room with some of my people — William Caughie or —— "

"No," said Isaac with decision — "I've been owre lang by mysel' to neighbour wi' William Caughie. What I cam to speir was the rent ye micht be seekin' for Betty Inglis' bothie?"

"Good. The place is, beyond contradiction, going to wreck. You are welcome to it, Isaac — we'll not quarrel about the rent."

"Na, I want nae back-spangs," Isaac replied.

"Oh, well, let us say a couple of pounds a year; or better still, you'll give me a few days during springtime in the manse garden."

"I'll gie ye twa pounds," said Isaac, "but let's niffer aboot the garden-work efter-hin."

Isaac stepped out into the fresh afternoon air with new hope. He knew of at least half-a-dozen gardens in which he could get occasional employment, with the prospect of ampler reward than was likely to fall to him from his new landlord.

The candle-maker was resting on the parapet of the bridge, conversing with the carrier, as Isaac descended from the manse. The former was expatiating to the latter on the cleverness of a perambulating radical, named Parlane, who had held forth to the villagers the night before in the large room of the Wheat Sheaf inn. The carrier had not been present, but he knew something of the man.

"A man o' great pairts," Brough had designated him inconsiderately.

McLennan was not prepared to endorse this eulogium without qualification, but admitted that the orator was a "cool haun. Dod, we could a' speak fine if oor minds were cool," he said. "Think o' the ideas that pass through yer ain head, but what comes o' them when ye want to put them in words? A cool man's mind is just like that pool when there's no wind. He looks into it, and sees the ideas just as ye can look into the watter doon there and see the reflection o' that bank wi' the crocuses, thae bare branches, and the red bricks o' the bleach-field wa'. You and me could spout lang enough if oor heads were as clear as that. To say what ye see doon there is as plain as reading 't oot o' a book, but wait till a scuff o' win' comes —— "

"Man, McLennan, that's awfu' fine," cried the candle-maker. "The scuff o' wind aye comes when I get to my feet, and blots oot every deil-haet I'm gaun to say —— "

The discussion was interrupted by the gardener's passage over the bridge. The carrier had told Brough about the sale of Broomfields, and now Isaac was able to augment the information by naming the purchaser. The three men there and then came to the conclusion that the doctor was going to marry the governess, as Mrs. Lonen had said. Under the stimulus of this fresh theme they sauntered up the road as far as the change-house. McLennan's sister was out delivering parcels, and the candle-maker's wife, owing to the sudden change of weather, was confined with rheumatics, so there was no hurry. The carrier, moreover, was a sympathetic man, and wished to give Isaac a consolatory dram.

What followed later in the evening, while part and parcel of the gardener's plan, would probably not have taken practical shape so soon but for this accidental adjournment. In Kilspindie there was a code of honour in connection with treating uniformly observed by the independent mind. When the company was large this was fraught with danger to the units that formed it. Whatever their practice might be in paying off other forms of indebtedness, in convivial moments the debt of a dram was liquidated on the spot, by a dram all round. Though this company was not large, when the darkening fell, it proved to be large enough, for as the two men got to their feet, and Isaac essayed to follow, it was found he had lost the use of his legs. His mind was perfectly clear, but inebriation had paralyzed his nether limbs. His companions assisted him up the brae, and told Mistress Izet that the body had "taen a dwam."

"Eh, my," she cried, hooking on the kettle, "I'll no say but he has got his death o' cauld, for he was sweatin' at his work like a brock the day. Think o' that; and the place sell't to them 'at'll no thenk him for 't. Will I rin for the doctor?"

"Rin for the doctor nane," Isaac commanded.

"Na, the doctor 'll be here sune enough to claim his ain without your sendin' for him," said McLennan — thinking of the purchase. "Get him to his bed, and pit a het jaur till 's feet."

With this safe advice, the two men, having discharged a neighbourly duty, withdrew.

Isaac sat in the cosy chair, and stretched out his gnarled fingers to the glowing fire.

"It's a peety," he remarked, as he watched the housekeeper filling the jar, which she corked tightly and buried at the foot of the kitchen bed.

"What's a peety, Isaac?"

"That I canna gang up to my ain bed."

"Dinna fash aboot that, ye'll be as weel here." She went to the parlour press, took out the family decanter, which had not been unstopped since the funeral, and brewed a stiff glass of toddy. "Noo," she continued, "drink this like a man, and then get awa' till yer bed."

"And what's to become o' you?"

"I'll sit up wi'ye. It's maybe a shock, and ye'll need hauns aboot ye."

Isaac smiled grimly.

"Janet, ye'r a trumph," he said; "and it's maybe just as weel I hinna the power o' my legs, or I michtna bide to tell ye a' at's on my mind. I've had the thing often at the root o' my tongue afore, but I aye daunert aff or it cam to the bit. Bring me a gless."

"What are ye wanting wi' a gless?"

"Never mind; bring't here and sit doon. Noo ye maun tak' the big hauf o' this toddy yersel', for I've had three drams already; and to tell you the truth — the honest truth, Janet — I'm leg-drunk."

"Oh, Isaac."

"It's true; my knees are like some auld macheen that has wrocht kina jachelt; but my head's richt clear. By the man, I never crackit like this in my life afore!" he cried, cracking his thumbs.

"Then it's no paralis?"

" Hoot, woman, paralis, no. I had the same thing on the nicht o' Willum Ringin's waddin', but a sleep among the clean strae brocht my legs to their senses. As ye ken, I'm no used to the whisky; but the carrier and the candle-makker meant weel. Janet, I've thocht a real heap frae first to last."

" Deed have ye, Isaac, and I've often wonnert what ye were thinking," she said, raising her eyes, while her lips parted modestly, wondering what was to come.

" And I have as often jaloused that ye kent. Janet, it's late i' the day, and there's no use o' us palaverin' like young folk. We have been like brither and sister for many a year. Ye have washed for me, darned and clooted for me, made my bed and tidied up the hoose, but this canna gang foret langer unless ye become my wife. What do ye think o' that?"

" Deed, I think it's a gey sensible-like thing," she replied calmly.

" Then that's a bargain," he said, wetting his thumb.

" It's a bargain," she said, putting her thumb to his, " if ye dinna forget it the morn. A thing o' the kind ance happened in Houston parish when —— "

" That's no likely noo," he interrupted; " the hoose is taen."

" What hoose? "

" Bet Inglis' bothie."

" Keep and guide us, did ever onybody hear the like o' that? And ye never let on."

There was no sentiment wasted at this betrothal. They drank their toddy, and had an hour's sensible talk about ways and means, at the end of which they agreed to exchange beds for the night. Mistress Izet thoughtfully brought the lobby bell, and placed it on a chair within his reach.

" Ring it lood," she said, "if ye need me," then she assisted him to the bedside.

" Efter a', Janet," said Isaac, with a twinkle in his eye, " it's a peety ye should leave yer ain bed."

" Ye auld futar," she cried, with a laugh, seizing the candle and running off to the door. "I micht 'a sleepit in my ain bed a' my days, and you in yours, gin yer legs had cam hame sober."

CHAPTER XIX

NATURE'S NURTURING AND PAIRING TIME

THE wine-coloured tassels of the flowering currant, as yet unaccompanied by leaves, drooped healthily under a gentle rain. Elm and chestnut trees were bursting into leafage. Even the tardy ash was awakening under the pressure of inward nourishment, but there was not a shimmer of green as yet among the network of branches. Against the milky back-ground of sky, however, there stood forth dark, tightly-shut fists of life, whose fingers would unfold by and by, and hold out a soft palm-like hand to the sun and rain. The brown earth of the fields was seen as through an emerald mist, with straight lines of deeper green, where the harrow-tooth had given strength to the nurturing soil. For weeks the lark had been heard over Coultarmains, and the cushet was already pouring forth his five love-notes in Crosby Glen. It was nature's replenishing and pairing time, when the invisible forces above and beneath work towards summer; and the awakening impulses of love and hope begin to stir in the human breast. While sitting in his own pew Willie Mitchell's eye caught Bell Cowie's as the minister proclaimed for the first, second, and third time that there was a purpose of marriage between Thomas Maughan and Lizzie Colquhoun. The whole congregation might have been gazing at Bell without seeing anything peculiar in her glance at the moment. The congregation, however, was not in love. The magnetic message he felt was for him alone, and taken in conjunction with the time and circumstances it thrilled him into such ecstasy of absent-mindedness that William Caughie, thinking the young man had got "cauld and was hard o' hearing!" touched him on the shoulder from behind with his horn specs, and whispered reverently that the text was in "Matha seeventh and fourt." Mitchell mechanically turned up the passage, but heard nothing of the elaborate chastisement which the preacher administered to his flock. The young farmer had frequently met Bell since that fair-day in autumn, when she incautiously promised to give him an answer in a twelve months' time; and while he never failed to show that his regard for her was as true as ever, he kept his conversation on the honourable side of the compact. Bell herself was rather tired of waiting for proposals. The utter dearth of these left her already biassed mind free to think more and more of the one open to her. Protracted thinking on one subject is known to narrow the mental horizon, but in this case the affections went arm-in-arm with meditation, the final result being that the only male person seen on the horizon was Willie Mitchell. Her mother had contributed in a kind of passive way to this consummation. Mrs. Cowie's aspiration for a marriage with Mr. Congalton had undergone considerable modification since the death of his daughter. She did not know of his engagement to the governess, but she felt that his removal abroad and the subsequent sale of Broomfields rendered his return to Kilspindie exceedingly doubtful. Since he had resisted all her own persuasive skill, the library, and Bell's charms, she thought it unlikely he would ever marry. Consciousness of failure left her gloomy and reticent. Bell, meantime, was allowed to dream her own dreams, and nibble the sweet cake of her own knowledge in secret. But Mrs. Cowie could not long remain in ignorance of how matters were drifting in the absence of competing wooers. Her daughter's tell-tale face was too ingenuous to conceal her feelings when her lover was near, or when his name was mentioned in her hearing. Mitchell, on the other hand, acting on Bell's advice, was always on his guard in Mrs. Cowie's presence. Since Congalton had eluded her, and no other star was in the firmament, Coultarmains appeared to her as not such an undesirable match for Bell. But what if he also was growing indifferent? Men could not be trusted for constancy. She sought her daughter's confidence with such unwonted kindness of manner that Bell told her all.

"And ye said ye would gie him an answer in a twelvemonths' time."

"Yes," whispered Bell, not daring to lift her eyes.

"That was richt prudent o' ye."

She recalled the proposal Mr. Sibbald had made. Probably it might still be open to them to accept it. If so, her daughter would yet have the half of Dr. Congalton's money, and marry the man of her own choice.

" Willie Mitchell is a weel-principled lad," she said. " It is true your edication and manners fitted ye to be ony gentleman's wife; after a' ye may perhaps find as much happiness in a farmer's kitchen as in a gentleman's ha'. But haud Willie Mitchell to his bargain for the present, and if things can be arranged within a year he'll maybe no have to wait a' that time for his answer."

Was the glad light that flashed in Bell's eyes from the front seat of the loft the offspring of this welcome assurance? The interview between mother and daughter took place on the previous Saturday afternoon, and had left behind it in the girl's heart a radiant memory. When they met after sermon-time Bell was bright beyond her usual, and winsomely coquettish. Mrs. Cowie saluted the young farmer with uncommon warmth, and then stepped solidly on with her husband. Had Mitchell decreed to take the most direct way to his own farm he would have passed the road leading to Windy-yett, and taken the next turning. Indeed, it had been customary for Mrs. Cowie, if he was of their company, to stop and practically dismiss him here with, "Weel, ye'll be steppin' foret." On the present occasion, however, the farmer and his wife turned into the loaning without even looking round. Mitchell thought this was exceedingly opportune, for he had something on his mind to say to Bell — a secret it was, in the meantime — the disclosure of which might lead to confidences more suited to this quiet path than to a public road thronged with home-going friends and neighbours. Bell paused at the turning with a testing gleam of humour in her face.

"Na," he said seriously, "I'm going on; I've something to tell ye."

"Something to tell me?" she inquired, looking up in his face soberly now. "Is't some ill news?"

"Weel, I can hardly ca' it by that name."

The light faded in Bell's eye. Was he going to give her up? Was he also — this indispensable factor in her life, about to dis-

solve into a shadow? He did not keep her long
in suspense.

"My sister is leaving Coultarmains."

"Leaving — have you quarrelled?"

"Na, she's getting merrit; but it's a secret
yet."

The colour returned to Bell's lips, and her
teeth sparkled as she replied —

"Deed, Willie, I thought by your face ye
had met wi' some misshanter. Wha is she
getting?"

Bell's boarding-school manner and speech
came and went with circumstances. A homely
farmer liked the vernacular best.

"Peter Main, the teacher at Kingsford. He
has been seeking her for a while, and they have
settled it at last; it's no to be named to onybody for a month yet."

Bell walked on a short space in silence. But
thought is rapid, and defiant of time. Susie
Mitchell and she had been school-fellows under
Mr. Lonen at the parish school. Susie was little
and plain, with rather a sallow complexion, yet
she — Susie — had attracted the attention of an
educated man; Peter Main, however, had dis-

covered qualities in his sweetheart that were to him before outward comeliness of face.

" And when is't to be? " she inquired at last, baffled in thinking of the inscrutable ways of men.

" Lammas," he replied. " It will be gey awkward for me wi' the hairst just beginning. Bell, will ye let me put foret the nock? "

" What do ye mean? "

She was rather a shallow young person, this Bell; neither mother-wit nor boarding-school education had taught her the significance of figurative language.

" I have promised no to speak to ye of marriage for a year," he said, " and I would have kept my word even in the changed circumstances, but I thocht frae the glint o' yer ee as ye looked at me frae the laft the day, that ye micht let me speir your answer earlier."

Bell held down a crimson face to hide its joy. His heart was still true to her. But what was this had taken his head — this " glint " he spoke of? Had she revealed prematurely to the sharp eye of her lover the transport she experienced at her mother's altered attitude towards himself?

" Tell me this ony-wye, Bell," he remarked, rather desperately, " do ye like me ony waur than when I first spoke o' marriage to ye?"

" No," she replied, with emphatic readiness — " far better!"

He drew a long breath of the nourishing spring air, then their eyes met.

" Bell," he said rapturously, " that's gran' news — wi' that answer I could maist wait oot the year."

They were nearing the farm; she laid a hand quietly on his sleeve, and spoke modestly and low.

" Ye'll maybe no have to wait sae lang, Willie. I'll tell ye mysel' when the time comes, but dinna you say anither word till I gie ye leave."

Mrs. Cowie and her husband had paused at the gable-end, and were contemplating with satisfaction a brood of raw-framed turkeys that had come into being during the preceding week, when the young people came up flushed and confused with their love-talk. Bell ran into the house at once, seeking shade from both outward and inward heat.

" Will ye no step in and rest a minute out of the sun?" Mrs. Cowie said, in her most engaging manner. " I declare it's like a day in June."

Mitchell thanked her, but gave signs of proceeding up the loaning. His heart was too palpably in his face, and his feelings at the moment were not in harmony with the commonplaces of farmyard talk. He required solitude, air, and largeness of prospect to encompass this wealth of pleasurable emotion. He was scarce out of earshot, so incomprehensible are the antics of lovers, when he commenced to whistle a psalm tune to unreasonably quick time. The leafy hollows of Endrick wood were vocal with the liquid notes of a wooing blackbird, but the grey lark of love in his own welkin was drowning all other sounds with palpitating melody. Further on he put his right hand on the top of a double-barred gate, and leaped over with the agility of joyous health. Before him, at the other side of the field, stood Coultarmains. The old steading, with the fleecy column of smoke above the kitchen chimney, and sheltered by the protecting arm of a bourtree hedge, seemed already to smile with the radiant presence of Bell.

CHAPTER XX

FATEFUL INTELLIGENCE

ON the morning of the day on which Isaac
Kilgour and Janet Izet entered their humble
dwelling on the glebe land as man and wife,
Richard Cowie, dressed in his Sunday clothes,
drove through the village on his way to Airtoun.
His object was to induce Mr. Sibbald and Dr.
Congalton's trustees to revert to the arrange-
ment which, a few months before, his wife had
instructed him to decline. For days he had been
irresolute about the journey. He had even confided his doubts to the smith, who agreed with
him that the plan could not now be carried
through in Mr. Congalton's absence; but Mrs.
Cowie held that a majority of the "daers" was
sufficient to settle the matter, and the stronger
will at length prevailed. No one, however, was
prepared for the news which Windy-yett brought

back with him in the evening. He blurted it
out in a sentence, as his steaming horse paused
for an instant at the smithy door. The candle-
maker was at a funeral in a neighbouring parish,
and was not there to hear; then he extended it
more respectfully to Mr. Lonen, whom he saw on
the other side of the hedge, as the horse zig-
zagged leisurely up the brae. "It's most mortal
a'-thegether," the smith had exclaimed, striking
his thigh. The school-master struck his spade
deeply into the earth as a specific mark of exclamation; uttered some phrases of academic
horror, and ran out the back way to convey the
news to the manse. Disregarding the ruts in
the loaning, Cowie sped on to Windy-yett at a
pace reckless of springs and wheels, and casting
the reins to the "orra" man, jumped to the
ground and made hurriedly for his own door.

"Lord keep us, Ritchie, have ye been drinking?" cried his wife, whose portly presence
entirely filled the space he essayed to enter,
casting her eyes the while from his feet to his
flushed face.

"Congalton's droont," he exclaimed, disregarding the unjust insinuation.

"Droont," she reiterated, her human heart getting the better of all selfish considerations. "Lord preserve us, Ritchie Cowie, are ye telling the truth? Puir man! How cam ye by sic news?"

"Weel, ye see, when I gangs owre to Airtoun I finds Mr. Sibbald in a bonny wye. He was gaun oot in a gey hurry. 'Excuse me,' says he, 'tell your business to my clerk, for I have just received news of poor Congalton's death.' 'Death!' quoth I, but before the word had richt left my tongue he was roun' the corner."

"Save us — and did you tell your business to the clerk?"

"Na, no likely. I said I had come to speir for Mr. Congalton, but his maister had directed me to him for particlars."

"My sang! that was wisely dune — ye never did a better thing. Weel?"

"'Oh!' says he, 'there's no particlars. The telegram cam frae the newspaper office only an hour syne — here it is — "Congalton drowned, letter and newspaper following with fuller news."'"

"And wi' that ye left?"

"Wi' that I left," he said.

Mrs. Cowie returned to the dairy to make up the butter, and her husband retired to divest himself of his Sunday clothes. Her feelings were so mixed that she did not care just then to reveal them even to her husband. Nan Pinkerton's forecast of news from the sea had proved true. She tossed and slapped the butter into prints mechanically. Her mind reverted to their last interview after his daughter's death. He was pale and thoughtful, but "ceevil spoken by-ord'nar." She remembered how he was dressed, and how the bonny diamond ring on his finger sent glints of light through the room as he moved his hand. "That too would gang to the bottom wi' him; maybe his body would yet be found"—she was thinking half aloud— "but thae heathen black folk would never send hame a valuable thing like that. Droont!" she said audibly, "puir man; and Bell micht have been a widow. I was gey headstrong to get her married to a gentleman, but I'll never mislippen Providence again."

The sad news soon found its way to every ear in Kilspindie. The smith went across and told it to the candle-maker on his return.

Tinny Walker, seeing the solemn crack and the long faces from his corner window, left his soldering-bolt in the fire and hurried to the Brig-end. Jimsy Waugh heard it when he came over from Millend for threepence worth of dips. M'Aull the twister, and William Caughie were busy setting a new web, when Mrs. Caughie, who had been " owre the gate strauchtin Nancy Beedam's hindmost bairn," came in and told them something was " gaun through hauns " at the Brigend. And so the neighbours gathered, " speired," and, for a space, speculated, then hurried homeward to break the monotony of their uneventful lives with this fateful news.

" That'll be gey sair bit to the pair on the kirk brae," Zedic Lawson remarked to his wife when they had mastered composure.

" Ser' them richt," she replied unfeelingly; " them that could belittle their ain relations. They were unco big aboot their allooance, but they'll maybe no carry sic a high head noo." These remarks referred to Isaac Kilgour and his wife. Mrs. Lawson being the senior, wished to see her sister married " wice-like under her ain roof." Isaac, however, did not like her officious interference. He bore it for a time, but kept his own counsel till the banns were proclaimed. Mrs. Lawson believed in a Friday's marriage. She would draw upon Janet's savings for such " needfu' cleeding " as Zedie and she required, and make an appropriate feast.   Isaac never let on, but secured the services of the carrier and his sister, went up to the manse on the Tuesday, and returned with his wife to their own small house on the brae for a " touzie tea."

Zedie sat for a minute with his mouth pursed as if whistling a tune, not yet having forgot the slight that had been put on them.

"Yes," he said, "cock them up wi' an allooance.   They canna think that we'll be vexed for them, for they did a real illset thing."

A copy of the London paper came in due course.   The notice of the striking event it contained was copied into the local weekly newspaper.   It told that the brig *Minerva*, of Panama, sailed from that port on Sunday, February 28, under the command of Captain Pierre de Linkskie, with a cargo of oil and canvas for Callao.   Her burthen was about 114 tons.   The crew consisted of seven persons, including the captain and his son, a boy twelve years old. She also carried a passenger named Congalton, a representative of an English newspaper. At three o'clock on the Monday morning, a week after their departure, they were forced to heave to in a gale of wind. Lying under close-reefed maintop-sail, and balanced reefed mainsail, a heavy sea struck the vessel and she suddenly capsized, turning completely over bottom up. The only person on deck at the time was the mate, named Bradford, who was instantly engulphed in the ocean, but on coming to the surface he was fortunate in getting on some floating wreckage. Supporting himself in the lee of the wreck, he passed the night and most of the next day, when in the afternoon a small coasting steamer hove in sight, and he was taken on board. They passed a hawser to the *Minerva* and took her in tow, but during the next night the gale freshened, the tow-line had to be cut, and the wreck was left to the mercy of the sea.

"Mr. Congalton," continued the *Despatch*, "whose untimely fate we regret to announce, was one of the most reliable and energetic of journalists. His experiences as our war correspondent were recently given to the world in book form. He went out to Peru as our special commissioner to watch over events in connection with the rupture between the Spanish Government and the South American Republic, and landed safely at Colon, but missing the mail steamer at Panama he evidently took passage on board the ill-fated *Minerva*. He was a man of kindly nature, infinite resource, and unbounded courage."

The candle-maker and the carrier got the local weekly between them at a reduced rate, when it was four days old. Zedie Lawson borrowed it and read the account of the incident to his wife. After the wedding she had made up her mind never to darken her sister's door again, but the resolve gave way — not on the side of magnanimity.

" I'll step owre this meenent," she said, " and read this to the pensheners." She went out and had gone as far as the manse when something occurred that altered her intention, so she stepped up and called on Mrs. Caughie instead.

Mrs. Caughie was a tall woman with a stoop in the shoulders. She was reckoned very "skilly in weans' troubles," could " greet " with the best, and was indispensable when there was a death in the house. In the main she was a helpful woman to the neighbours. Her manner was funereal, and she spoke with a " sneevel." Mrs. Caughie occupied a higher platform than Babby Lawson, because her husband was an elder and Zedie Lawson was not. The latter, moreover, was but a gingham weaver, while William wove gauze. Still, Babby Lawson had the assurance to go into any society when she had news to tell. The incident that had diverted the latter from her purpose was that as she went round by the kirk, the governess, dressed in mourning, alighted from a carriage that had driven her to the manse brae, and "sailed doon" to her sister's bothie.

" Dressed in mournings, said ye? " inquired Mrs. Caughie, with so much interest that she upset the cog on her lap into which she was grating potatoes to make starch for her husband's linen.

" Ay, dressed in mournings," she replied.

" Was it deep? "

" No dead deep — a black gown, a bonnet wi' a bit crape, and a black veil."

" Did ye no follow and get the news — she'd have something to tell? "

" I didna need nae news; the paper here tells a' that's ever likely to be kent."

" Ay, woman, William was reading that. It's a sad story. To think he hadna an hour to mak' peace wi' 's Maker. It's said he never darkened a kirk door, and that he wrote godless stories and things on the Sabbath day. It's like a judgment, but there's maybe some private message; the governess wouldna drive a' the way here for nothing. Ye should have followed in, woman; but I suppose you're no great wi' your sister. Did she no speir ye to the marriage ? " Mrs. Caughie had heard Lexy McLennan's version of that story, but wanted to get it from the other side.

" Marriage ! " she replied, in a tone that showed how strong her feelings were, " did ever ye ken the like o't? To think that they should march up to the manse wi' the carrier and his sister, when they had the hoose o' a near relation to get married in — I feel black affrontit." Mrs. Caughie's knotted fingers were busy with the grater. " I'm tauld it was that dour ettercap Isaac, but, my certie, he'll no carry sic a high head, noo that the allooance is stopped."

"Isaac's a queer craitur, and has wyes o' his ain," was Mrs. Caughie's guarded reply.

"What are ye saying aboot Isaac?" inquired the gauze weaver, coming in with stealthy step, his thin nose shining like a cameo under the pinch of the fresh wind.

"We were just talking aboot the deplorable end o' his late maister, and aboot his and Janet's allooance being stopped."

"Allooance," he reiterated, "they're better off than ever. Miss Hazlet has been owre to Kilspindie wi' a message from Mr. Sibbald to say that Mr. Congalton has pensioned them baith for life in his will."

Mrs. Caughie gazed at her husband with a doubtful, questioning look.

"But, William, didna the minister tell ye the doctor's siller would gang to the Cowies if he dee't?"

"So he did, but the man had siller o' his ain." William pushed the horn specs above his eyebrows, walked to the ben part of the house, and settled down to his loom. Was he, an elder of the kirk, going to "palaver wi' a backsliding clypin' woman like Babby Lawson — no like."

CHAPTER XXI

SETTLEMENTS

PETER MAIN, the teacher at Kingsford, was over at Coultarmains, spending the week end, and had to make an early start on Monday morning to be in the school at ten. Willie Mitchell having a commission from his sister took down his gun, put the powder flask in his pocket, and convoyed him as far as Moorburn Toll. There was a dewy freshness in the fields. A soft rain was falling with gracious and reviving gentleness. Over the near landscape there seemed to come a sough of bursting life — a sensible stirring of summer energy in the misty greenery of wood and lane. Mitchell on his return, was tempted off the highway, and got a couple of rabbits while rounding the upper shoulder of Ferleigh Glen. The rain had ceased

by this time, and the sullen canopy overhead
parted revealing spaces of azure, from one of
which the sun made sudden emergence, giving
gem-like radiance to the raindrops on the grass.
He mounted the stile and took the mossy foot-
path through the wood. The sun was shining
warmly now on the blossomed gorse; spruce
and larch, with dripping tassels of tender green,
spread their protecting fan-like branches above
him, cooling the air with their graceful motion.
The path was strewn with the ripe brown fruit
of the fir. On either hand daffodil, primrose,
and may-flower held up prophetic heads with
morning freshness. An early starling with
a lobe of the earlier worm swinging from its bill
ran defiantly across his path, eagerly regarded
from above by the expectant brood. But
neither beast nor bird, flower nor tree, engaged
his thoughts. He was thinking soberly just
then, what a change it would make for him
when Susie went down to the school-house.
His step grew more elastic and a light came
into his eyes, for his thoughts had darted
forward under the quickening influence of hope.
Bell loved him, and had spoken encouraging

words — but he must wait. His lengthening step, impelled by the energy of health, carried him swiftly down the mossy slope to the high arched bridge, under which the black water from the upper moorland was increasing its pace for a leap over the linn. Further down, this hissing and plashing flood filled the branchy chasm, then plunged into the rocky caldron beneath. Thus dreaming with bent head, and the gun barrel, upon which he had slung the rabbits, on his left shoulder, he reached a sudden turning of the path where the road dips deeper into the glen. Was there human magnetism in the air? His dreams gave place to the consciousness of a living presence. Behind the dripping branches of a bonny broom, golden with blossom, he caught sight of the swaying drapery of a fresh print gown, and ere he knew, he was face to face with eyes that widened with welcome, and unmistakably glad lips that smiled.

"Bell," he exclaimed, his own heart leaping to his eyes with answering joy. At the same moment she cried, "Willie," and both expressions meant the same thing — unspeakable, unexpected pleasure. Bell had no need to be admonished to smiles now, for love itself brings the best expressions of beauty to the face.

"Whare have ye been so early?"

"The ploughman's ill," she replied. "I was doon at Glenside speirin' for him. Your a guid bit oot o' your ain gate."

"I was convoying Peter Main a piece, and then I took a turn round by Ferleigh to get a couple o' rabbits for Susie — she's aye at a loss for Monday's denner."

Bell was looking up at him with admiration, this tall, weather-bronzed giant with the happy hungering eyes. Something in her look encouraged him.

"Bell," he said with subdued rapture in his voice, "I never saw ye looking sae bonny." She struck him playfully on the arm with her small empty basket, lighter now for her visit to the ploughman's bothie, and turned aside her head to hide the increasing colour. "I wish—" her happy eyes were back to his face expectantly.

"What d'ye wish?" she inquired encouragingly.

"Oh, there's no use wishing," he replied; "I maun be patient, my lips are sealed."

"Willie," she said solemnly, then pausing—the situation was delicate. She plucked a spray of broom and commenced to undo the patient efforts of nature, by pulling the golden blossoms to pieces. Her face was rather serious, and the long brown eye-lashes seemed to be lying on her cheek from excess of modesty. But she drew heart of grace, his lips were sealed, but hers were not. "Willie," she repeated, as if the liquid syllables afforded her pleasure, "I told you it might not be so long — and — I would let you know when you might speak."

"Yes," he said eagerly, "weel? — weel?"

She was contemplating the bottom of her basket now.

"If ye are still o' the same mind — I — I — think ye might speak to father and mother now."

"And, Bell," he had taken both her hands in his, "are ye sure what their answer will be?"

"I think the answer will be — yes," she said.

.   .   .   .

When Mitchell returned to the farm, his porridge was cold; and Bell's mother saw plainly that some happy circumstance had "taigled" her daughter by the way.

Mrs. Cowie had not been idle since the news of Mr. Congalton's fate reached Kilspindie. After a reasonable pause she had herself driven over to Airtoun to find out their rights from Mr. Sibbald. The lawyer admitted that her daughter's claims on the late Dr. Congalton's estate were absolute. He was preparing a statement, which would be laid before the trustees probably by Martinmas, or as soon after that date as possible. It was not to be thought of, however, that she would leave Bell's affairs entirely in the hands of men who for aught she knew, might in spite of the minister's assurance, help themselves freely to her daughter's money. Accordingly, like a woman of prudence, she engaged a solicitor and directed Mr. Sibbald to account to him. In the next place, she took Bell into her confidence and told that young lady frankly of her fortune. That it all legally belonged to herself, but that morally she and her husband had certain claims on it for her upbringing, her expensive education, etc., which claims, the heiress frankly admitted, "There will be enough efter-hin to mak ye a catch for the best gentleman i' the land, or for that matter, to

mak ye independent o' men a' thegether." Bell
had been led to believe that her own natural
attractions were sufficient to bring gentlemen of
birth and education to her feet, but so far they
had failed to come. Moreover, she had no wish
to occupy the proud position of being altogether
independent of a man. In her then frame of
mind, she did not see that such suitors as might
be tempted by this fresh inducement would be
worth waiting for. In fact, Bell had indulged of
late in so many day dreams in which the cheery
and industrious farm kitchen had a place that
the thought of a "fine leddy life" had now no
charms for her. Besides, had not Willie
Mitchell loved her for herself alone? His love
was entirely disinterested, for he had sued for
her hand before it was known such good fortune
was in store for her. Mrs. Cowie's matrimonial
ambitions had been frustrated; she had even
humbled herself so far as to admit that Providence had acted wisely in so doing. Notwith-
standing, the ruling passion in the woman's
nature was hard to extinguish. Bell was
eminently fitted to be the wife of a superior
man. She was not so over-mastering now with

her opinion, but she advised Bell after her
return from Airtoun, to take a week to think
about it. Bell was dutiful, and obeyed, but the
result at the end of this period was that her
mind was more and more made up. She had
given continuous consideration to the question
night and day, but the time was absorbed in
rosy dreamings of farm life, of well-stocked
byres and golden stack-yards, how bow-windows
could be struck out here, and improved outhouses according to recent reading, erected
there. She would have a garden laid off ever so
much nicer than they had at home, with a
green-house where they could grow vines. Then
in the lownest and prettiest nook of this garden
enclosure there would be a summer-house with
a porch up which creepers would grow to keep
her in mind of the place where she first learned
how strong and deep and unselfish the love of
a man could be. The outcome of this serious
consideration of the matter was known to her
mother for some days before the accidental
meeting with her lover in the glen.

The exigencies of the season made it meet
that the young farmer should remain in the

fields till the day's work was done; but the metaphoric wings Bell had placed on his heels enabled him to "lowse" early. His reception at Windy-yett later was cordial, but business-like — cordial in so far as the consent to marry Bell was concerned.

"But there maun be settlements," said Mrs. Cowie. She had talked the matter over with her husband, who remonstrated feebly. If there was to be any business talked she must do that herself; he would not interfere in the matter, "buff nor styme."

"Settlements," the young man repeated, not quite comprehending, for being unmercenary he had not thought of the necessity of such legal terms, "Od, I hinna thocht aboot nae settlements, a' I cam for was to ask your leave to settle doon wi' Bell."

"Prime," laughed Windy-yett with unbecoming levity. Mrs. Cowie's look, however, checked his merriment.

"It's no laughing matter, but serious business. If ye kent mair ye would jest less. It's what is common in the best society, and Bell is fitted to marrow wi' the best. It is true we have agreed to her marriage, but the siller maun be settled on hersel'.''

"When I sought your daughter," Coultar-mains spoke with frankness and spirit, "I kent nothing aboot this siller, maybe we'd have been happier withoot it, for I've seen the like; do what you think right aboot settlements for it maks nae differs to me. We have enough to keep us as it is, and a' I want is Bell." This delicate but all-important duty having been settled to her satisfaction, Mrs. Cowie was disposed to make concessions in matters of less weight. Mitchell wished the marriage to take place as soon as possible. His sister was leaving him at Lammas, and with the harvest coming on, it was desirable that he should not be left without a housekeeper. Mrs. Cowie was too practical not to admit the reasonableness of this wish.

"I vote that the twa weemen be knocket aff at the ae time," the farmer remarked with forgetful jocoseness. The light-heartedness was untimely. His wife reminded him severely that such language was ill-fitted for the occasion of

her daughter's marriage, being more descriptive
of an "unction mairt."

The idea of Bell being married side by side
with Susie Mitchell!

"Na, na," she said firmly, thinking of
the mixing of relations, "we'll have no double
marriages. Bell will be ready before Lammas
gin ye like; but as for the marriages themsel's
we maun be content wi' ane at a time."

CHAPTER XXII

NANCE M'WEE'S CONFIDANTS

NANCE M'WEE, the dairy woman, as she was called at Windy-yett (the name, however, covered but a fraction of her duties), had a way of saying things to herself that sometimes gave her relief. The orra man helped her as a rule at milking-time, and when there was butter required Mrs. Cowie occasionally put to her hand. But she had cheese to make, the washing to do, and such cooking, between times, as the family required. Nance had come to Windy-yett three years by-gone without a character, and when Mrs. Cowie was in a mood not to be too particular about other people's feelings she was none loath to cast it up to her. This misfortune arose out of a misunderstanding. She had been in a town place previously where a neighbour servant was kept. This girl was from the Highlands and had unusual ways. One day she fell in the scullery and twisted her back.

" I will lie down on my face," says this Highland girl, "and you will stand on my back and bring it right."

Nance, willing to be useful, did as she was told, but being a stout lass there ensued a succession of deep sonorous nasal exclamations that reminded the operator of what she had once heard from a gaelic pulpit on sacrament Sunday. Thereupon the mistress came in. Poor Nance's place on the neighbour girl's back was misunderstood. The mistress being sentimental called her a " horrid woman." She had previously intimated that as soon as the fires were off she intended to keep only one girl. This incident settled her choice — Nance must go — she would stand by the girl who had been trampled on.

Nance did not like the town. " The scenery wi' drunk men on a Setterday nicht," as she confided to the orra man "was just awfu'." Her desires were pastoral. She liked the soft eyes and balmy herbal breath of the cows, and never wearied of ministering to them. She was a good sort — Nance, and very willing to work;

but since the marriage was fixed, as she confided to the wash tub, "the day wasna hauf lang enough for what there was to do. Everything is dune in sic a hurry that naething is dune richt. The mistress is that unreasonable and gets into a pucker aboot naething. Just think o' her raging into my room at fower on Monday morning crying oot, 'Nance, Nance, get up ye lazy woman, the morn's Tuesday, the next day's Wednesday, the hauf o' the week gane and no a turn o' work dune yet.' There noo, I declare ye wud think I was amphibious and could be in twa places at ae time." Nance hurried away from the washing green at her mistress's call, and addressed her next remarks to the frying-pan.

"I'm no losing my memory nane, as she thinks, but I havena fower pair o' hauns. It's gey hard that she should be so snappy to me and so fair to thae dressmaking women ben the hoose; but they flatter her aboot her taste, her style and what-not, and tell her that a woman o' her position should have this, that, and the ither, till she's clean blawn up wi' vanity. They tell me it a' comes o' this lash o' siller she's gotten by the droonin' o' that gentleman she was so set on for Bell. But what's siller guid for if it doesna bring rest and contentment to the mind?"

Nance hurried off to set the dinner in the parlour where the women folk were working among their silks, laces, and other bridal paraphernalia.

"Table naipkins!" she came back to the kitchen to say. "Did ever onybody hear the like o't? 'Nance,' says she, quite calm-like, 'ye've forgot the table-naipkins,' as if ever I had seen table-naipkins i' the hoose before. Then she gangs owre to the drawer and feches oot some fine towels, opens them at the fold, and cocks them doon, end up, beside each plate. No doot it was a reasonable enough thing to gie the women something to dicht their greezy fingers on so that they wudna fyle the things they were working wi'; but to blame me! It's a mercy I didna break oot and tell the truth. But Bell looked up and made a face at me — she is real decent that wye — as much as to say 'Nance, it's a trying time, but just you thole till this is by!'"

It was indeed a severely testing time for poor Nance during the six days the dressmaking went on, but she always found solace at evening milking time. The walk home through the clover field with the cows and her communings with them afterwards was the one compensating experience of the day.

As Nance set off thoughtfully round the end of the byre to fetch her dumb friends in to the milking you might have fancied she was admiring the sunset or the soothing bird-melody in the neighbouring wood; but no, her heart was in her ears listening to the lowing welcome of the cattle. She knew the distinctive call of each, "That's 'Daisy' or 'Becky' or 'Buttercup,'" she would exclaim. Then as she reached the gate and put her shapely arm through the bars to undo the hasp, she would address the half-dozen moist noses about her shoulders, "Puir leddies, have ye been wearying for me?" Day by day she had something new to tell them, as the creamy froth rose higher in the luggie between her knees. When the orra man was there she spoke in general terms. "Beware o' siller, leddies." She was in a didactic mood, "Na, I needna name nae siccana thing to you, for ye wudna ken what to do wi' siller though ye had it, puir things, but siller whiles does mair hairm than guid, putting upsetting notions

in folk's heads, making them rideec'lous baith
in their ain station and in the station they aim to
fill. But, leddies, you're no to think that siller
honestly come by is a bad thing. D'ye hear
that, Danny lad? siller's guid if ye ken hoo to
use it. Mony have heaps o't that are no rich
ava, for they hinna the hert or winna tak' the
trouble to do guid wi' 't. They only get their
meat like the rest o' us, puir craturs, and a
cauld bed i' the kirkyard when a's dune. But,
leddies, gin I had siller I wud big ye a new
byre, and buy a silver bell for the neck o' ilk
ane o' ye. Ay, wud I; and ye wud sleep sweetly
at night on a bed o' clean pea-strae. Then I
wud send Danny here to the college, and mak'
a minister o' him; and when he got a kirk I wud
gar him tell me wha was in trouble and I wud
gang and help them wi' my ain haun." The
prospective minister having been summoned
from the byre to run to the merchants, the confidence became more personal. "But heigh-ho!
Daisy, my lass, I am but a poor servant like
yersel' and barely as weel used. Here, even
withoot a character, as the mistress never fails
to remind me, though I'm sure ye dinna heed

aboot thae things so lang as ye have kind
hauns aboot ye." Nance was summarily called
from the milk-pail to find her mistress inveigh-
ing against slackness, and Bell in hot, but
unsuccessful pursuit, of a brown hen whose
restlessness had got the better of her maternal
instincts. On returning she resumed her monologue, breathing rapidly, "Danny must have
left that door open, though as usual, it was
blamed on me. Ah, leddies, learning and pump-
slippers put folk fair oot o' place in a farm-yaird.
Boarding-schule edication! I wonder what guid
a boarding-schule edication dis ye if ye canna
catch a clockin' hen. I declare I'm clean breath-
less wi' that race. Na, Daisy, my dawtie, I
wudna have tholed it so lang but for you and
the ithers. Though if, gin this marriage is by,
there's no improvement — weel, I winna break
your kind herts by talking aboot what might
happen at Marti'mas; but as my decent auld
faither used to say, ' better a finger aff than aye
waggin'.'"

Nance was in better spirits at a subsequent
milking-time.

"This is the last day o' the dressmaking, and,

leddies, from what you've heard tell, I don't think onybody has reason to be sorry, for though the women were guid shewers they gied us a' a hantle o' work. But Becky, lass, ye'll no guess what I'm gaun to say — I got the present o' a new goon for the marriage. Yes, a new goon! Na, ye needna look roon for it's owre braw for the byre. But Sunday eight days is my day oot. If you're at the laich end o' the meadow-field keep your ee on the road as the folk come hame frae the kirk, but I assure ye you'll need to keep a sharp look oot or ense ye micht mistak' me for a fine leddy. Eh, it was an uncommon nice thing o' Mistress Bell to think o' the new dress. She took me aside and said her mother had come through an anxious time, but she wud calm doon and a' wud come richt when the marriage is bye. Eh, my leddies, gin that cam true it wud be guid news."

Two nights before the wedding the hearts of the bovine audience were fluttered by mysterious confidences; though the whisperings at times could not have gone much beyond Becky's well-elevated and back-turned ears. " Oh, leddies, I have something to tell ye, but ye maunna let on.

It's weel for you that Danny's no here, or ye
wudna get a syllable o't frae me. But it's a
secret, a dead secret, and if ye werena sic great
friends I wud keep it to mysel'; still-an-on it's a
comfort to have ye to speak till. I wis up at
the junction station yestreen wi' a message frae
the mistress, and I forgathered wi' somebody,
but ye wudna ken his name if I tell'd ye. He's
connected wi' the railway, and drives about in a
great iron carriage that wud fricht ye to see, but
he's unco quiet and kind himsel', and I've kent
him sin' ever he cam' to the junction, and — and
— noo when I think o't, I maunna tell ye the rest
yet, just tak' time and try to mak' oot the leeze
o' the thing among ye; and, leddies," — Nance
raised her voice that all might hear, "if ye find
oot the secret dinna vex yoursel's aboot me, for
if it's ony comfort to ye, ye should ken he has
got a bonny bit cottage — and a coo."

Whatever Nance's secret was, even the beef-
witted listeners might have identified her friend
as Jaik Short the engine-driver on the Junction
Railway. Jaik was a widower with two pretty
little mites of children, and as Nance had said
he was possessed of " a bonny bit cottage and
— a coo." 293

CHAPTER XXIII

BELL COWIE'S WEDDING

ISAAC KILGOUR had a three days' job at Kil-baan, but on the morning of the fourth day important news arrived, and Miss Hetty Hazlet gave him an early dinner, charging him to convey the intelligence with all haste to the Manse of Kilspindie. It was a lovely morning in the last week of July — the day on which Bell Cowie was to marry Willie Mitchell — and everybody thought the sunshine was a good omen. Isaac started with ordinary activity about noon, but, for reasons of his own, did not wish to reach Kilspindie in a hurry, so when he got round the elbow of the road he went leisurely. It was four o'clock when he reached the point where the Garnet comes in view, four miles from the manse. He might have been at Kilspindie by that time with moderate walking. Isaac left the dusty high road, took a sheltered loaning leading to the river, and settled himself on a thymey seat at the tail of a pool where the sun was making liquid honey-comb above the gravel. On the opposite side a clump of marsh-mallows, with great yellow cups, leant down to the edge of the still water, and doubled its beauty. Flies flickered in swarms up stream, their shadows darting here and there on the amber bottom, deceiving the fish with unsubstantial fare. The gardener was curtained from the heat by kindly trees. A balmy wind coming down the valley rippled softly across a field of wheat, and toyed with the blue-green tassels of the firs on the opposite bank. Isaac appeared to be counting the moving dots of fleece on the green hill-side beyond the clover meadow. But who can tell the ferlies that may pass through the mind of a taciturn man, or gauge the mystery of his thought when he never lets on? He had mused and rested an unreason-able time for a person charged with urgent news, and was apparently half-dozing when the smooth water beyond the willows was violently split, and a great bull-trout leaped in the air, shook a

stubborn head, and fell back with a sonsy splash.
The spectator was no fisher, nor did he know
the ways of fish; but on turning his head to
watch the rings of the pool widening towards
the shore, he saw something, like a fine wire,
slicing the water in different directions. Following this upwards, for the sun was gleaming
on it, he observed above the intervening willows
the graceful bend of a strong rod, whose rings
and joints glittered in the light. He was interested mildly, but did not alter his posture.
Once again the captive fish sought unavailing
freedom in the air, but the unseen fisher handled
him with absorbing skill, and it was not until he
had laid the fish on the grassy bank, and contemplated the prize from different standpoints,
that he observed Isaac.

"That was a game fight," he cried over the
water, proudly. "He's a beauty — six pounds
at the very least." Then he lifted the captive
by the gills displaying his solid shoulders and
speckled sides, as if challenging the spectator
or the light of day to take an ounce off the
liberally estimated weight. Indifferent people
take things for granted to save concern. Isaac

nodded, and turned away, but next moment
he was conscious that this well-dressed sportsman was ploughing across the swiftly-running
stream with a goodly-sized flask in his hand.
Isaac watched the young man pensively as he
splashed towards the bank on which he sat.
He might be admiring the generous social impulse of the youth, but more probably he was
wondering who had made the money — his grand-
father or his father — which had paid for that
flashing diamond ring, and that faultless outfit
he wore.

"By Jove!" (he spoke with an English accent,
nobody swore by those foreign gods in these
northern by-ways) "that is a fine fish! Don't
you think so? At any rate you must drink my
health." He stood in the water and poured a
libation that would have cheered the heart and
been welcome to most men in the gardener's
station, but Isaac remained seated and shook his
head.

"No!" exclaimed the young man in honest
surprise. "It's the best old brandy; no questionable stuff; has been in our cellar for over
twenty years."

Perhaps Isaac concluded it was his grand-
father who had amassed the money; they
generally made ducks and drakes of it in the
third generation, but he said simply —

"I canna stand it, sir. I wish ye weel."

"Ah," said the fisherman sympathetically,
"head easily touched?"

"No," replied Isaac; "it's the legs, and I'm
fower miles frae hame."

The youth laughed good-naturedly, drank the
old man's health, emptying the cup. "It comes
of drinking that coarse national liquor of yours.
I knew a man who was addicted to it; but nature
in him was too gentlemanly, preferring to break
down rather than be brutalized. You Scotch
people know nothing of the delights of respectable inebriation. Champagne, followed by a glass
or two of green Chartreuse, is the right thing,
makes you comfortably magnanimous; if you
are impelled to move, your motions are dignified and graceful, and there is no feeling of fiery
discomfort, no sudden angular impulses of pro-
pulsion, such as one sees to be the result of
your masterful Scotch whisky. By-by." The
bibulous philosopher waved his hand, recrossed

the stream, and stalked gaily down the mossy bank on the opposite side. Isaac watched the pliant top of his finely-balanced rod twinkling above the willow branches after the fisher himself had disappeared.

"Daidlin ninycompook!" was all the gardener said. It was a home-made phrase, but served his purpose. He looked at his watch; whatever the record of time might be, it seemed that as yet there was no immediate necessity to move on.

All the afternoon there had been uncommon stir on the roads converging on Kilspindie. You could stand in front of the candle-maker's workshop and see the farmers with their wives and daughters (the sons found their way on foot), driving from south and west towards the scene of the afternoon festivities at Windy-yett. Those from the south passed over the bridge, while others, journeying from the westward, could be seen over the low hedge as they drove along the high road above Nancy Beedam's cottage. Harlaw, Sheersmill, Damhead, and William Purdon, the laird of Drumlaw, had all passed with their belongings, and waved their whips in jovial salutation to the group of male gossips at Brig-end. William Lonen closed his school an hour earlier than usual, and after posting a sonnet to the editor of the county newspaper, he and his wife got a "cast foret" in Harlaw's gig. Harlaw was a well-to-do bachelor, with a bien farm, and that day many a glance had been bestowed on the looking-glass, and many a delicate touch given to the feminine toilet with him in view.

Everybody said the smith should have been invited, though some who made that remark considered they had an equal claim, and meant simply to provoke an expression of his disappointment. It was a sore point undoubtedly, but to the outer world he passed it off with grace. "There is sic a fell heap o' relations," he said modestly. At home, however, there was a different story.

Windy-yett, a month before, was over at the village consulting the smith about a "coo-beast" that was threatened with pneumonia. Without due consideration of his limited rule at home, he had told Mrs. Pringle that she maun practise her steps for a skip at Bell's wedding. Where-

upon there was a great stir in the smith's household. His wife made several discoveries. Indeed
she was appalled as she turned out the wardrobe
and exposed her things to the light of day. She
had a cloak that was fashionable when Jenny
was at the breast, but Jenny was now five years
old. Her silk gown had been turned, and looked
"sair tashed." She would not say a word about
her bonnet. It was bought after the roup at
Smiddy-yard, but she could get sprays, and a
yard or two of cheap ribbon, and put them on
with her own hands. That surely was economy
sufficient to satisfy any man. But what man is
there gifted enough to be reasonable in matters
of female attire? When the smith inconsiderately asked if "the gown wudna turn again,"
she laid the things meekly past, and said it was
"clean nonsense in her state o' health to think
o' gaun to onybody's wedding." The smith said
nothing more at the time, but this was the point
at which he always gave in. He made up his
mind that a new gown she should have — at least.
Meantime his wife went about her duties meeker
than ever, and kept on expressing the hope that
they wouldn't waste an invitation on her. Never-

theless, for days before they were issued, she contrived to be about the Brig-end every morning as the postman passed.

"It's a cruel shame!" her husband exclaimed two days after Mrs. Lonen had shown her invitation to Mrs. Pringle. "They're nane slow to seek us when they want a favour. Ritchie Cowie should have held his tongue aboot dancing at Bell's wedding."

"It wasna his faut," his wife replied gently. "Besides, it'll save expense."

"Save expense!" he reiterated with reckless benevolence. "Wha cares for expense? — it's the affront! I was gaun to gie ye a silk gown, woman, but ye's get a new jacket too, and appear at the kirkin as fine as the best o' them."

"You're aye that kind," his wife replied with tears in her voice; "but ye manna think o' the jacket, Peter, we never could afford it. Besides——" She hesitated.

"Besides what?" the imperious husband demanded.

"I'd be braw an' proud o' a silk goon," she said, looking up in the grim, kindly face; "but dinna think o' onything mair, for a new jacket wud belittle the bonnet."

"Dagont!" he cried, striking his great black fist on the dresser. "I am so angert at their treatment o' us that ye'll get a new bonnet as weel, to spite them!"

"Oh, Peter, hoo could I ever gie in to that? — But you're sic a maisterfu' man."

Thus the affront was alleviated. It was agreed, however, on the suggestion of Mrs. Pringle, that they should defer making these purchases till after the wedding lest any one should suppose they had been provided for that occasion.

In the grey of the evening Kirdy's cairn, behind the change-house, became the absorbing point of interest. Here a tar-barrel and various inflammable faggots had been built into a compact pile, to which the younger and gayer spirits were adding the finishing touches. The more amorous and seriously-disposed swains took their places under the great chestnut-tree at Elsie Craig's well, where, in company with fresh and winsome maidens, chaperoned by "water-stoups," they could improve their time while waiting for the bonfire.

Isaac Kilgour turned into the loaning leading to his own house as the candle-maker gave the word of command to fire the cairn. This distinction naturally belonged to a man who had sacrificed a score of his rankest "dips" to speed on and intensify the conflagration. Zedie Lawson crept past his brother-in-law under the obscuring shadow of the hedge as Isaac went down the brae. He wondered if the mean whistling body had been at the bothie after the spiteful things he and his wife had been saying about their marriage. Janet was standing at the door, looking up between the hedges.

"Has he been in?" Isaac inquired.

"Na; the craitur wud be sent roon to spy ferlies. He's aye snokin' aboot. Come awa'; I have your supper ready."

Isaac went in and deposited the red pocket-handkerchief containing his travelling requisites on the small settle.

"Couthie Janet — irr ye there? — Come ben Isaac," cried the bird above the girnall, then its muffled voice ran into a cynical cackle of a laugh. Isaac turned, and was making for the door when his wife intercepted him.

"You're surely no gaun oot again wi' yer supper on the table?"

"I maun see the minister," he said doggedly. "I'll supper nane till I've seen the minister."

"But the minister's at the marriage."

"The marriage will be bye an hour syne; he doesna bide for the dancing."

"Then ye'll have ill-news, I'se warrant. Is onybody ailing?"

"Bide awee and ye'll hear; the news is no that ill."

It had occurred to her that she had seen "just sic anither dour man in Houston parish," when he pushed past her and walked leisurely up the loaning towards the manse.

From inquiry at the door he learned that the minister had not yet returned, but was expected immediately. The fire was now blazing nobly on Kirdy's cairn. The inn, the school-house, Broomfields, and the cottages between were smitten with the palpitating glow. The smithy and the candle-maker's workshop lay in comparative gloom, save when the flame lengthened fitfully, and caught sight of the red-tiled roof. The gleam from the cairn bridged the river from hedge to hedge, lit up the loom shops on the right, and travelled on towards Millend, revealing the votaries at Elsie Craig's well, adding its cheerfulness even to the kitchen-gardens where the privet hedges were not too high. The merchant's modest one-storey building had no share in the rejoicing warmth owing to the masterful prominence of Tinny Walker's gable. It was not long before Isaac's expectant ear caught the crackle of wheels above Broom-fields. Then he heard a few voices in the neigh-bourhood of the inn initiating a cheer which gradually spread until it was taken up by the larger concourse of villagers surrounding the cairn. This cheer was in honour of the minister, who, before the echoes were done with it, had reached the manse gate.

"Are they marrit, sir?" said the gardener, coming out of the shadow as Mr. Maconkey stepped down.

"Ay, Isaac; I've fastened a hasp the day they'll no unbuckle in a hurry."

"There's no doubt aboot it in a legal sense?" persisted Isaac.

"The case is beyond doubt both legally and

morally," laughed the minister. " But, Isaac, you are excited. Is there anything the matter? "

" Na," he replied, " there is nothing the matter wi' me; but I have news for ye. Noo that the marriage is bye, ye may preach it from the pulpit or the hoosetaps gin ye like, for it's richt gled gospel news — Mr. Congalton's saved ! "

CHAPTER XXIV

THE RESCUE

ASTOUNDING as it may appear, the intelligence which Isaac Kilgour carried so tardily to the minister of Kilspindie was true. The circumstances, when they came to be fully known, formed a romantic chapter in real life stranger than fiction. When the *Minerva* so suddenly encountered that terrible onslaught of sea and wind which shifted her cargo and turned her over, all on board were below, as has been told, with the exception of the mate, who escaped and communicated the intelligence of the disaster on his arrival in port. Captain Pierre de Linkskie, his son Nicolas, and Congalton were in the cabin, while the remainder of the crew, consisting of four men, were in the forecastle. After the vessel was overturned and escape rendered, as it appeared, impossible, the captain succeeded in wrenching open the trap hatch in the cabin deck, thereby liberating some casks that were jammed in the lazarette, where also provisions were stored. Having effected this, he scrambled up into the vacant space, taking his son along with him. He afterwards assisted Congalton to follow. Meantime a terrible fight for life was being waged in the forward part of the vessel, in the midst of which one of the men was drowned. The other three, by seizing hold of the windlass bits, succeeded in getting up close to the keelson, and so kept their heads above water. Finding that the upsetting of the boat and the consequent displacement of the cargo had started the bulkhead, they contrived to draw themselves along the sides of the keelson towards the stern of the vessel, where they heard the voices of their fellow prisoners. Six individuals were thus closely cooped together in this limited space, submerged to the waist in the sea. They were able to distinguish between day and night by the light being reflected up through the cabin skylight, and thence into the lazarette through the trap hatch in the cabin floor. Two days and two nights thus passed without food, without sleep, and almost without hope. They endeavoured to assuage the pangs of hunger by chewing the bark stripped from the hoops of the casks, but want of renewed air threatened them with death by suffocation. The captain laboured almost incessantly for these dreadful two days, endeavouring to cut a hole through the hull, but happily his knife broke, before he succeeded in accomplishing this thoughtless task, the result of which, had it been successful, must have proved fatal to all, as the confined air alone maintained the vessel's buoyancy.

On the morning of the third day, ere it was light, the derelict was struck heavily, so they supposed, by a passing vessel. As a result of this shock, another of the poor fellows fell into the hold and was drowned. The stern began gradually to droop, and they thought all was lost. The displacement of air in the lazarette forced them to move forward, in attempting which the boy, who was by this time half dead from the vitiated air and want of food, missed his footing and was seen no more. The absence of motion excited hope that the vessel had grounded. In a short time they were sensible that the water beneath them was subsiding, and after an hour or two of terrible suspense, the captain ventured down into the cabin. Part of the quarter-deck had been stove in, and as the water receded, fresh air soon reached them, and revived the spirits of the imprisoned men. Then they saw through the riven timbers with unmanning joy the rosy flush of dawn breaking on the land. Applying such implements as they could lay hands on with all their remaining strength, they cut their way through the opening which had been made in the quarter-deck, and found that they were stranded on one of a small group of uninhabited islands in the vast Pacific. Fortunately the unavailing attempt which had been made to capture the disabled vessel, had left them in the drift of the providential current that carried them to land. A week's unspeakable privations on this inhospitable island passed ere their signals were observed by a passing steamer by which they were picked up and safely landed at San Francisco.

The news of the miraculous escape, briefly

stated, was conveyed to London and Kilbaan by the same mail, but it was not till Congalton's return that the details, as now recorded, were fully known. This "Romance of the Sea" linked as it inevitably was with Dr. Congalton's legacy, and the interesting local events arising out of it, sped its course widely over the world's highways, and interested many there, as well as in the by-paths of this small northern parish.

Mrs. Cowie held up bravely for two days, but on the third took to her bed. It was believed her husband spoke under inspiration when he informed the candle-maker that she had "slippet her fit and got a kina shake to her system." The public mind, however, was not to be over-ruled by such machiavelian devices, for every-body knew she had taken to bed over the loss of the Congalton siller.

There was a select party of three in the candle-maker's workshop. The time was evening, and the door was shut that they might have fuller license of speech. A frame of candles that had received their final dip was suspended over a vat of coagulating tallow. The candle-maker, having given up work for the day, was

seated on an inverted barrel, while his two companions sat with their backs to the westering
sun on the bench near the window. The colloquist on the barrel had just told of Windy-yett's
remark as to the cause of his wife's illness, and
wondered who had been the first to break the
tidings to her.

"It was the minister," the smith said. "He
got the news from Isaac Kilgour on the nicht o'
the marriage, and he had to gang owre to the
Haugh the very next day for Matty Semple
was in unco trouble."

"Trouble, said ye? man, I didna hear o'
that." The carrier was surprised for he had left
some delf ware at the Haugh two days before.

"Weel, ye see, I got it from William Lonen
in a kina secret, for the minister 'll no like it
named. Puir Matty thocht her kye had been
bewitched. It was blamed on Nan Pinkerton,
richt or wrang; for do what she micht the milk
aye blinked (turned sour). She had hung
horse-shoon on the byre-door, and put branches
o' rowan and bourtree roon' the wa's and even i'
the graip-hole, still — the milk blinked, so, at lang
and last, she beet to send for the minister."

" Weel? " the interested listeners queried.

"Weel, he let the body tell her story and listened patiently. Says he, ' Martha,' says he, ' it seems to me that the evil e'e has been cast, no on your cows, but on your dishes,' for he saw they were geyan dirty — ' tak' them doon to the burn,' says he, ' and let them lie there for a while in the running water, and then rub them weel wi' a clean clout,' says he, ' and when that is dune bring them in and pour a kettle-fu' o' boiling water on them, for boiling water is a thing the evil e'e canna stan'. When ye have them weel scalded, set them on their sides to dry, and I'se warrant your milk will blink nae mair,' says he."

" Man, that was rale humorsome o' the minister," cried the carrier. " I aye allowed the minister had humour, though it's no often he tak's oot the spiggot. I said the same thing to Jaik Short the ither day, but Jaik said if he had humour he must have a fifty-six on the safety valve."

" What did puir Matty think? "

" Oh, she took it perfect serious and thocht it was a charm. But I begude wi' Mrs. Cowie, and this leads me on. Weel, ye see, the minister being at the Haugh, it was but a step up the burnside and across the knowe to the Cowie's, so what could he do wi' the news in his head, but step in. Windy-yett himsel' was oot i' the lea-field helping to fit up a bothie for the Irish shearers, but his wife was at hame, thrang putting things i' their places after the turn up the nicht afore ! "

" I alloo it was a thankless journey. Did she break oot there and then? " inquired the candle-maker, anxious to get on.

" No then — and this is the queer bit o't. The minister thocht she was gratefu' to a bountifu' Providence for sparing Mr. Congalton's life, but efter-hin when Windy-yett cam' in she yoket on him, as Nance M'Wee could tell, and blamed him wi' this and wi' that, telt him it was a' through his slackness that Mr. Sibbald hadna arranged for their getting the hauf o' the doctor's siller — she would do this and that, and, so on — gang to the law and spend their last shilling, but she would have the richts o't."

" So she just angert hersel' into her bed?"

The candle-maker was partial to immediate sequences.

"That is no doubt true," replied the smith, "but isn't it a mortal thing to see hoo a woman's temper never fully gets the better o' her till she meets some object weaker than hersel'?"

This was a problem in feminine ongoings the carrier had no skill of. His sister, who was his housekeeper, had no temper to speak of, never having been flattered into arrogance by a man. The other two, thinking they were the stronger vessels at home, could look abroad and pass strictures. The smith's wife, finding at an early stage which of the two had the stronger will was wont to break in tears on the iron front of her husband and get her way. The candle-maker admitted that it was "a puzzle a'thegether. Marriage," he said, "was a double harness. A man and his wife might yoke fair to start wi', but by and by they were sure to rin tandem, for the stuffy ane was aye bound to work to the front." He had no dubiety in his own mind that he was the "stuffy ane," for his wife had long been in poor health — yet she ruled him by importunity from the invalid's corner.

While they were inwardly congratulating

themselves that they had not lost the reins like Richard Cowie, they heard the sneck of the door lifting, and the long spare form of William Caughie entered. When William was excited, he generally wore his horn glasses above his eye-brows. He had also a way of "thrawing his mouth," and working his attenuated nose to one side in the pause of making a remark, as if he was shaping an interrogation. What he had to tell was that the mistress of Windy-yett had taken "a terrible turn — a shock or something," and that Ritchie had come "owre for the doctor in a terrible pickle." William could have diagnosed the case to his own satisfaction, for he prided himself in having a "by-ord'nar" knowledge of the human structure. But on this subject he had once been rudely, as he thought, taken to task by Tinny Walker.

"William," the tinsmith said, "ye have a michty wye o' speaking aboot the organs, as ye ca' them, in folks' insides, as if they were great machines. Man, ony doctor will tell ye they could a' be set up and hae plenty o' room in an ord'nary hat-box."

For his size William considered Walker the "upsetten'ist man i' the parish," but he felt the rebuke. On this occasion he only suggested his suspicion that there was " something no richt about the hert."

" Or the brain," supplemented the carrier, " if it is a shock."

" Or the brain," William admitted, " a strain on the nervous system — that would tell on the brain, as like as no."

Bell and her husband returned from their honeymoon sooner than was expected. They had heard the remarkable news of Congalton's rescue in Edinburgh, and had calmly talked over the consequences to themselves, of this event.

Mitchell was a strong, independent, self-reliant man, who vigorously detested the thought of waiting for dead men's shoes. His strength of character had already impressed Bell, who was now more concerned about her mother's condition than her own monetary misfortune.

" Let us get hame to the harvest," the young man said bravely. " I'm nane vexed aboot your loss, Bell, for it canna be a great thing to lose what ye never had. The man's life's safe, and that's better than siller; honest work and health are great blessings, and wi' these we'll find enough to do us withoot pinch, and there's this comfort, Bell, my lass, what we mak' wi' oor ain hands 'll no turn oor heads."

CHAPTER XXV

THE SPAE-WIFE AND HER CUPS

ALEC BRODIE, the cartwright, lived about a quarter of a mile from Kilspindie, at the junction of the crossroads. The situation was such as to command the work of two parishes. The building of which he was proprietor was of one storey with a frontage to two roads. He and his family lived in one end, and his workshop and wood-yard were at the other. Behind the house there was an elevation commanding the west, on the top of which grew a few scraggy fir-trees with a strong inclination northward. This was locally called the "Hill of Man," but William Lonen, who was skilled in topography, said the name was originally "Helmend," resembling as it did the hindermost part of a vessel. The light growing dim in the

workshop, Alec had retired to the Hill of Man
with a book. He was a great reader, a scholar
his wife called him. He was known at times
to write verses — he drew the line at sonnets,
thinking of the school-master — but books could
not be read nor verses made in a small cottage
literally overflowing with bairns. He did not
at once take to his book, for he was thinking
of work that might probably require to be done
before morning. The near landscape, lined with
grey dykes, and fringed at intervals with trees
and hedges, was blurred and dim, but, having
the poetic temperament, he was beguiled into
strange imaginings by what he saw beyond
the line of the material horizon. The sun itself
had disappeared, and in the wonderful after
glow there was sufficient to afford diverting
interest to an imaginative mind. The dark
and distant margin of wood and moor seemed
to constitute the near boundary of a mighty
sea, while a remote bank of cloud, well up in
the heavens, served the fancy for a horizon.
What a fairy picture for a homely man, but
nature is no respecter of persons. She opens
her picture galleries and her concert chambers

impartially to all who have eyes to see and ears to hear. The cartwright was enraptured with this mysterious liquidity of colour, this primrose softness, varying in tone from salmon-tint to lightest azure. There were capes and islands, purple and rosy with sunset, great bays fringed with golden sand, and argosies that might be freighted with the treasured glories of oriental climes. Towards the nearer shore, marling the straw-toned water, long streaks of wavy grey rolled inward, and in combination with a light intermittent wind in the pine-trees over the cartwright's head, completed the illusion of motion and sound.

"Most mortal," he said, thoughtless of the incongruity of the exclamation, "I ken fine it's no real, but it's terrible naitral-like. A body never could put that sea-picture in words; but if I was an artist I'm thinking I'd have a bash at it wi' a brush. After a', when a body thinks o't, the colours were never made that could clap doon on paper or canvas either, the onspeakable beauty o' a scene like that." He turned to his book — it was already almost too dark to see, but he had read the passage

before he left the workshop, it had struck his
fancy —

> " As doctors give physic by way of prevention,
>   Mat alive and in health of his tombstone took care;
> For delays are unsafe, and his pious intention
>   May haply be never fulfilled by his heir.

> " Then take Mat's word for it, the sculptor is paid;
>   That the figure is fine pray believe your own eye;
> Yet credit but lightly what more may be said,
>   For we flatter ourselves and teach marble to lie."

.   .   .   .

Brodie had accidentally come across a selection
of old Matthew Prior's poems, and being, from
the exigencies of his business, in the under-
taking line himself, it was natural his fancy
should go out to a man who had such provident
forethought as to supply his own tombstone,
and take care that his Epitaph was honestly
carved on it, while yet in life. These reflections,
however, were broken by the approach of his
eldest son, whose head was seen in the dim
light as he waded up hill among the tall
brackens.

"Weel, Alickie," he inquired, stepping down
to meet him, "what's the news? Is she ony
better?"

"No; she's fast sinking, they ettle she'll hardly win by the turn o' the nicht."

" Did ye see Winny himsel'? "

"No, he was sitting owre his bible at the fire-en, but Nance tell'd me."

"Weel, laddie, we canna stay the gaun fit o' death. We maun be stepping doon to the shop — ye can look oot the strauchtin' brod, and I'll get the timmer put in order." He had a contract for the parish coffins at 13s. 6d. each, but this one could afford a fuller margin of profit. "It'll no hurry the puir body nane, Alickie, still ther's nae hairm in being ready for death when it comes."

The cartwright was a man of fine sentiment, but being the responsible head of a large and needy family, he couldn't afford it much indulgence when profitable work came his way. Brodie and his son sawed and planed till midnight, but no summons came — a " strauchtin' brod" for the poor shattered demented mind was what the mistress of Windy-yett required just then. As to the covering for her mortal remains, Alec Brodie need not have been in such oracular haste.

The crops had been safely gathered at the Mains, under favourable weather conditions. The harvest had been abundant, and the sun, well pleased with the completion of his work, was smiling out of the west on Willie Mitchell's well-filled stack-yard. Bell sat knitting alone in her sanded kitchen. A kettle was singing on the hob, and the black Persian cat in front of the fire lay winking with dignified satisfaction as it contemplated the antics of the kitten playing with the young housewife's worsted. The kitchen-maid had been sent over to Windy-yett to inquire for the invalid. Physically there had been a partial recovery, but the strong will was broken and the memory gone. Marriage and this home-trouble had sobered Bell. Her flightiness had toned down. She had come to understand by the patient teaching of her husband that happiness was an attitude of the mind arising out of a sense of duty honestly done. Providence had given her a comfortable home, the best of husbands, a sufficiency for all her wants, and she was content. At times her school days in Edinburgh, the girlish dreams of making conquests

and marrying into social position, stimulated
by the inordinate ambition of her mother, came
back to her mind, but only to convict her of
folly. Could the artificial atmosphere of society
in which, from her superficial education and
rustic training, she was ill-fitted to live, afford
her the solid and simple happiness she now
enjoyed? In her clean sanded kitchen she
could receive her country friends and neighbours like a queen. In the drawing-room
both she and they would have been out of
place, ill at ease, and — such things have happened — she might have been coward enough
to be ashamed of them and their ways. There
was a matronly seriousness about the plump
comely face as these reflections flitted through
her mind. Then she smiled, for she remembered her poor mother's injunctions. She had
smiled many a time to order, but the resultant
conquest happily, as she now thought, had
not been made. What lasting happiness could
come of conscious acting? Her husband had
been drawn to her before she had thought of
him as a lover. Indeed, and this made her
wonder, it was when she showed the greatest

indifference that he became most vehement in his attachment. How delightful, she thought, for the lover to find out when he became a husband, that his wife had a reserve of charms; but what must it be in the severe disillusionment of married life when the actress has been found out? Bell raised her eyes from the twinkling wires and gazed out of the window with softly parted lips. The wistful face was beautiful. Her eyes, dreamy and expectant, wandered over the foreland of heath and furze, and the grey stubble of shorn fields, to the long white ribbon of a road that lay beyond. This was the way by which her husband would return from Kilburnie market. She did not really expect him for an hour yet, nevertheless her hungering eyes had several times traversed this meandering road fondly, as if to anticipate her own expectations. A shadow darkened the window for a second, and passed ere she could focus her vision to the nearer object, next moment a small black-eyed woman, in a drab cloak that draped the figure to her ankles, stood in the doorway.

"Guid e'en to ye, Mistress Bell," said the visitor, dipping her body till the hem of her cloak touched the doorstep. The apparition was Nan Pinkerton of the Haugh.

"Good-evening," replied Bell with a slight look of trouble in her eyes. The house-maid had told her that Matty Semple blamed her neighbour, the hen wife, for casting the evil eye on her cows. Bell had said she did not believe it. Only people who were without education fancied such things; yet she did not appreciate this visit all alone by herself in the gloaming. Bell had known Nan from her own childhood. She was peculiar, reserved, and made pretence of sibylline knowledge. She was excommunicated by the Rev. Dr. Someril for spae-craft and contumacy, after spaeing Beeny Wauchops' fortune (Beeny was a light creature and went wrong with black Will Gibb the gamekeeper), but though Mr. Maconkey — Dr. Someril's successor, wished to restore to her the privileges of the Church, she refused to be reinstated. Nan was an authority on the concoction of herbs, and her specific for "chin cough" was believed in by not a few matrons in

her own and neighbouring parishes. In theory
Bell was not superstitious, but she was alone,
and it was as well to be civil.

"Wont ye come in owre and rest?" she said,
setting a chair with a straw-matted seat in front
of the fire. "Now that the harvest is in, the
evenings are getting cauld."

Nan in her moods had the abruptness of
masculinity.

"I had a dream aboot ye last night," she
said, "and cam' owre to drink a cup o' tea wi'
ye to see gin it be true."

"I hope it wasna an ill dream," replied Bell,
smiling only with her lips. The spae-wife was
silent for a moment, her dark glittering eyes
fixed on the glowing fire.

"Guid or ill, true or fause, I daurna tell till I
see it i' the cups."

"I winna grudge ye a cup o' tea," said Bell,
taking her keys and going to the corner cup-
board — "but" — should she tell her visitor she
did not believe in spae-craft? After all would
such a statement be absolutely true? "I'm
afraid I don't want my fortune told," was all
she said.

"Ay," remarked the Sibyl grimly, "ye have gotten your guid man, and think there is nothing in life worth kennin' after that; ye want things to go on as they are, but that canna be. Fortunes will whiles forecast themselves without our speiring. If my dream reads right ye have nothing to fear, but it maun be in your ain cup I read it."

Bell brought out the brown tea-pot and caddie with trembling curiosity. "Do ye like it strong?" Nan took the spoon out of the young wife's hand and measured the "masking;" then taking a little box from her pocket containing a whitish powder she covered a small silver coin with the mixture and shook it in on the top of the dry tea. Bell was then directed to half fill the tea-pot with boiling water, and set the cups. The rite was impressive in its ceremoniousness.

"A year syne I drank tea wi' your mother."

"Did she believe i' the cups?" inquired Bell in astonishment. She had never heard of such a thing.

"Ay she was in a hurry to forecast something that was in her mind, but, as whiles happens, the reading wasna clear, the same mischance aye turned up; something connected with the sea."

"Connected with the sea!" cried Bell, then she bit her lips and went over to the window. If the spae-wife herself did not know how fully that misfortune had been realized she would not betray the secret. Her poor mother! Bell was pale and her hand shook as she poured out the tea according to the directions of her guest. First the guest's cup was to be filled, then the tea-pot was to be shaken with circular motion from left to right, after that the person whose fortune fell to be revealed was to fill her own cup. They sipped the tea in silence. As Nan gazed thoughtfully into the fire a live coal fell on the hearth.

"Na, ye mauna touch it," exclaimed the elder woman, as Bell rose to replace it. "That's a coming guest that ye'll no wish to leave your hearth in a hurry. My dream is already half read, but we'll aiblins see the rest here." She lifted the cup which Bell had laid down, whirled the dregs round the sides, and then commenced her scrutiny of divination. The withered eye-

331

lids were puckered with a moment's concentration, but the wrinkles soon gave place to a look of satisfaction.

"It's e'en as I jaloused," she said; "I see your visitor coming doon frae the lift."

"From the lift?" cried Bell, "then it canna be man or woman either."

"It's neither man nor woman, it's an angel. I see ye baith lifting hauns till it wi' joy on your faces. There is gear and happiness to come — efter-hin."

"Oh, Nan," cried Bell, interrupting, "here's my husband." The wheels craunched sharply into the yard as Bell with crimson face rushed to the door. In a moment Mitchell had leaped from his seat, and taking his wife in his arms kissed her. "I have heard something ye'll no guess," he said, leading her towards the kitchen door.

"What?" inquired Bell rather flurried.

"Mr. Congalton has come back, and, disappointed no doubt that ye were beyond his reach, has married the little governess. Have ye visitors?" He paused at the door, catching sight of the spae-wife and the cups, then a visible shadow of displeasure settled on his face.

"It's only Nan Pinkerton," said Bell, "she has been bringing us good news."

"Ay," said the visitor, getting to her feet at the sight of the young farmer's frown, "men are owre wise to believe in auld wives' freits. I'm no welcome, I see, but I didna come up to the Mains to pleasure mysel'." Nan gathered her cloak about her, set her face to the door and disappeared in the gloaming. Mitchell's head fell on his breast as if stunned; then he took his wife again in his arms while his voice trembled with yearning solicitude.

"Bell," he said earnestly, "was this your seeking?"

"No, Will — no," she replied, seeing his meaning and trying to keep back the tears. "Nan came while I was waiting for you. She had a dream about us, and asked for a cup of tea. I couldna refuse, for I thought she was tired."

"I'm glad ye didna tryst her. What was her dream?"

"Some angel guest that would come wi' happiness for us baith — and gear." The young farmer looked at his wife with wistful tenderness. There needed no spae-craft to predict the probability of a welcome visitant, nature had told him that; **but the emphasis put on the gear** vexed him.

" It s the old story, Bell,' he said, putting his arm round her waist kindly, and smoothing her hair. " Some guid we hinna got that's coming. Oh lass, lass, we're gey happy for the present, but dinna put foret the nock as I ance asked leave to do, and try to force what's hidden from us. The wish to possess ither folk's gear has wrocht muckle ill. Thrift and work will bring a' worldly things we need, and happiness alang wi' them. Now," he said, holding her at arm's length and looking lovingly into the soft eyes that were ready to overflow with tears, " I'll put in the powny while you set the tea, and after that I'll tell ye a' aboot Mr. Congalton's marriage."

CHAPTER XXVI

CONCLUSION

It was late on a golden afternoon in the second month of autumn, a year after the events of last chapter, when Isaac Kilgour passed his brother-in-law on the road without recognition and climbed the hill slowly towards the kirkyard. He had a small basket in his hand filled with fresh-cut flowers. The gate to the sacred enclosure was massive and heavy. It had recently been donated to the parish by the laird of Templemains on the occasion of his being made an elder. It was curiously wrought and fashioned between two substantial pillars, and bore several suitable scriptural quotations amongst the fret-work of its design, "I am the Resurrection and the Life," "Dead yet speaketh," "Whoso believeth on Me shall never die," might be read with comfort by the spiritually minded, though to the sorrowing unbelievers, if such there were in the parish, these familiar texts could but add mockery to their grief. Isaac laid down his little basket, for it required both hands and all his strength to operate against the powerful spring intended to resist bovine curiosity and intrusion. The sacred acre was enclosed by a wall which on three sides rose but a few feet above the level of the graves. In the central space stood fragments of the old church with one gable and a window intact. Slabs of marble around the remaining walls referred in terms of affection to early pastors whose labours were closed. At the gable-end, a modern granite monument, with heavy protecting chains looping it to suitable corner pieces, testified that it was erected by a loving people to the memory of the Rev. Dr. Someril, "the sainted pastor of the parish." The mossy sward all around was ribbed with graves. Stones and slabs of varying sizes, facing promiscuous ways, and standing in various degrees of erectness, were scattered over the place, bearing local names — many of them frequently

written in this Chronicle. Isaac stepped slowly
and reverently over the mossy mounds. The
spot he came to visit was not seen from the
entrance-gate, having its situation off the west
side of the chapel wall. It was the sweetest
little space in the whole enclosure, level, turfed
with evergreen grass and closely shaven. This
soft, cool, well made bed, was strewn with
flowers tenderly laid there the day before, and
now again the reticent attendant had come to
perform the daily ministrations of "happing
his bairn" with flowers. At the head of this
plot there was an Ionic cross, delicately worked
in white marble, and set in thin graduated
blocks of red granite. The inscription carved
on the marble was simple — " Eva Congalton
aged 8." Then followed the words worked
into the circle round the cross. " Bless Thy
little Lamb to-night." Isaac gathered up the
discarded blooms and put down the fresh ones.
To him this was a sacred duty like saying his
prayers. As he retired a few steps to survey
the spot, his eye instinctively travelled from
the grave to the cross. " Her ain words, puir
lammie, as she lay doon weariet to her last

sleep." The gardener loved the stimulating influence of a pipe when in a thoughtful mood, but he would not smoke in the neighbourhood of this grave; he however sat down on the kirkyard wall to think. The master and Miss Hetty (it was them he was thinking of then) were now happily married, and settled in London, but they had left him and Janet "in chairge o' the bairn." He was thinking also in his own unlettered way that a well-developed sense is sometimes more helpful than genius. Hetty had written about her cousin Willie who was at last making his fortune in a tea and coffee plantation in India, not by mental gifts, but by the accidental discovery of an abnormal power of smell and taste. Miss Hazlet was married to the parish minister of Kilbaan, and her parents by her husband's desire returned to close the evening of their days at the old manse. The pension to Isaac and his wife had been indubitably secured to them. He could make more than his rent out of the manse garden by a few days' work in spring, so that there was no call to go afield, and certainly no employment would be accepted that interfered with his daily care of this little grave. Sitting there looking out over the village he was reminiscently happy. A column of blue smoke swayed on the still air above the smithy. A horse neighed at the door, and the hammer rang inside on the anvil. Several men sat apart on the parapet of the bridge and smoked. Tinny Walker (he was known by his size) had his shoulder close to the candle-maker's elbow, while the latter leant over his own half door with his hands clasped before him contemplating the wall of the smith's garden. Isaac's eye travelled up the village street between the colouring hedges towards Broomfields. It was the spot in all the landscape most pregnant with memories to him. William Caughie came out of his door to join the carrier as he passed leisurely down the brae, but to Isaac they were not consciously in the scene. His thought had the scope of many years and many recollections, embracing humour, sentiment of a kind, and tragedy, but in and out amongst the warp and woof of his musings there appeared the sweet sympathetic face of an unselfish woman, and the thoughtful prattle of an eager questioning child. The sun was more than half under the peak of the Baidlands, but it splintered a lance in the Holm woods below Kirdy's cairn, amongst foliage that gleamed with the pathetic beauty of decay. Nearer, the river stole beneath, mostly in shadow; at times its course was deep and slumbrous; anon leaving a pebbly strand on one side; it would swing brokenly under the shoulder of a protecting bank, caper for a space among the grey boulders, then thread the eye of the distant bridge, and disappear at last among the bent covered dunes. While Isaac sat a dog-cart rattled round the corner of the merchant's house, and caught his eye. He recognized it as belonging to Coultarmains. The appearance of this dog-cart had evidently provided him with a fresh train of thought, for he turned his head and his eye rested on the brown mound of a newly-made grave. Almost simultaneously the heavy gate was pushed gently open, and a youthful matron, dressed in black, stepped timidly over the intervening spaces towards the spot on which Isaac's eye rested, and, stooping reverently, she placed a

wreath of fresh flowers on her mother's grave.
Poor Bell — and yet, why poor? Two months
before the little guest, which Nan Pinkerton
had foreseen hastening to her from the "lift,"
had come and nestled cosily in her bosom.
Was she indeed an angel paying the youthful
couple only a passing visit? At present she
was daintily human, but whether she was to
develop wings and use them need not trouble
the reader of these closing lines; as yet the
wings were not even in bud. The small asser-
tive mite of a guest had come to count in the
census returns, while the active, masterful, well-
intentioned, but not over-prudent grandmother
had passed humbly within the kirkyard wall,
without knowledge of the advent. Bell whispered her mother's name. If she could but
know — oh, if she could see and apprehend the
joy which the priceless treasure had brought
into their home, she would forget all her disappointments. If she had been worldly, if she
had been ambitious, Bell felt it had all been
for her own sake. Now, when the truest and
purest happiness that earth could give had been
attained, she could only whisper her gratitude

to the inanimate earth. Isaac considerately took his departure unseen, while these regretful reflections were passing through Bell's mind. By and by she left the new-made grave. There are friendly visits to pay even in a kirkyard, especially here, where grave was linked to grave by friendly or neighbourly association. The grave of the grim but kindly old humourist whose last testament had bred such trouble was naturally suggested to Bell's mind by this visit to her mother's grave. From Dr. Congalton's place of sepulture it was but a few steps over the mossy grass to the small enclosure with the marble cross. This dainty spot, bright with the fresh flowers, had a tenderer interest to Bell now that she had a grave and a child of her own. She thought of the bright face and the clever English tongue, now, like the others, at rest beneath. Had her mother's wishes been fulfilled she might have been a mother to her — A mother? Bell wondered if that could have been possible now that she realized the intense love and self-forgetful tenderness she felt for her own child. Her reverie was broken by the sound of a voice at her side. On looking round she recognized the postman.

"I saw ye frae the road," he said, "and jumpit the wa'; it'll save me a walk to the Mains." The letter he gave her was addressed to herself, and bore the London postmark. Bell was nervously curious, and broke the seal where she stood. The writing was in an unfamiliar hand, and evidently difficult to read, but she spelled through it with her lips parted. Her face flushed and her eyes sparkled as she caught its purport. With the open letter in her hand, she ran with forgetful gladness to the grave on which her flower wreath lay.

" Mother — mother —" she whispered in suppressed intensity of joy, "all has come right at last — at last: " then frightened at the sound of her own voice and the odd eeriness of the situation, she hastened back to the road where the boy was waiting with the dog-cart, and drove quickly away.

When she arrived at Coultarmains, her husband was at the top of a ladder putting an armful of fresh thatch on one of the numerous stacks of oats with which the farmhouse was flanked on three sides, while her father, who had just returned from a neighbouring market, stood below shouting up the current prices of such agricultural stuffs as they were mutually interested in. Bell's heart beat fast, and her limbs trembled with excitement as she ran forward to salute her father.

" Come doon, Will," she cried, " and come in baith, for I have great news to tell ye." She hurried off, and when the men reached the house the young mother was on her knees, with head buried out of sight in the cradle, talking in broken language to a red wry-faced pigmy, into whose unwilling ear she was endeavouring to convey the idea that she would be a " michty leddy " yet.

" What's this great news, Bell ? " inquired her husband.

" Read that," she said proudly, handing the letter to Will. Then addressing her father — " Mr. Congalton has made owre his daughter's share o' the doctor's legacy to oor bairn."

" I thocht we had dune wi' that job," said Windy-yett shortly. " Whare got ye the letter ? "

" From the post lad." Then she lowered her

voice; " it was put into my hand *within sicht o'
the three graves!* "

The young farmer read the letter gravely, and
went back on certain portions of it, while Bell
followed his eyes, and tried to read the frank
but serious face. She remembered certain con-
versations that had taken place since their marriage regarding Dr. Congalton's money, and the
decided opinions he had held regarding it; but
while she endorsed his sentiments then, it was
now too apparent that the influence of heredity
was not wholly eradicated.

"Well," she inquired timidly, almost fearing
what he might say.

"It's a very kind and generous letter," he
replied slowly, " but as your father says I thocht
we had dune wi' this job. The doctor's siller
has brocht ill-luck and trouble enough already.
I'm real — real sorry to see you so built up in it,
Bell, for I thocht we had come to an understanding aboot it lang syne."

" But it's a gift," she argued, " no a legacy.
Besides — " (the tears were coming), " can we
refuse if it's a gift to the bairn? "

" There may be ither bairns," he said gently ;

"if that be sae let them a' be alike to us, we'll gie them what we can afford, and teach them sic notions as becomes their station. I'm sure you're far owre wise a lass to wish that this wee thing because o' the siller should grow up to look doon on the lave."

Bell gazed helplessly at her father.

"Willie's richt," he said, "no good can come to man or woman either by being pitch-forked oot o' their place."

"Bell is a kind and reasonable lass," her husband said, rising and kissing her. "We're richer in ae sense for this generous offer, but I'm sure when we come to talk the matter owre calmly atween oorsel's, Bell will agree wi' me in doing what is richt."

THE END.

www.ingramcontent.com/pod-product-compliance
Lightning Source LLC
Chambersburg PA
CBHW021750110726
47902CB00006B/1467